PENGUIN BOOKS

2025

MAIGRET AND THE HUNDRED GIBBETS

GEORGES SIMENON

GEORGES SIMENON

MAIGRET AND THE HUNDRED GIBBETS

*

TRANSLATED BY
TONY WHITE

PENGUIN BOOKS

Penguin Books Ltd, Harmondsworth, Middlesex
AUSTRALIA: Penguin Books Pty Ltd, 762 Whitehorse Road,
Mitcham, Victoria

—

Le Pendu de Saint-Pholien first published 1931
This translation first published 1963 in Penguin Books

—

Copyright © A. Fayard et Cie, 1931
Translation copyright © Tony White, 1963

—

Made and printed in Great Britain
by Cox & Wyman Ltd,
London, Fakenham and Reading
Set in Monotype Garamond

CHAPTER I

Inspector Maigret Commits a Crime

No one noticed what was going on. No one suspected that a drama was being played out in the waiting-room of the small railway station where only six depressed-looking passengers were waiting, amid the smell of coffee, beer, and lemonade.

It was five o'clock in the afternoon and night was falling. The lamps had been lit, but through the windows the German and Dutch Customs and railway officials could still be seen pacing up and down in the murk of the platform.

Neuschanz railway station is located in the extreme north of Holland, on the German frontier.

It is not an important station; Neuschanz is barely a village. No main lines pass through it. There are trains only in the mornings and evenings for the German workmen who, attracted by the high wages, work in the Dutch factories.

The same ritual is repeated each time. The German train stops at one end of the platform. The Dutch train waits at the other end.

The officials wearing orange caps and those in greenish or Prussian blue uniform meet, and together while away the hour's wait for Customs formalities.

Since there are only about twenty passengers on each trip, and they are regulars who call the Customs officers by their Christian names, the formalities are soon completed.

The passengers then go and sit in the buffet which is typical of all frontier buffets. The prices are marked in both *cents* and *Pfennigs*. A showcase contains Dutch chocolate and German cigarettes. Both gin and *schnapps* can be had.

It was close that evening. A woman was dozing at the cash-desk. A jet of steam was coming from the percolator. The kitchen door was open and you could hear a radio whistling as a child was fiddling with it.

It all seemed ordinary, yet there were a few odd details which were enough to make the atmosphere heavy with a vague sense of mystery and adventure.

The uniforms of the two countries, for instance; and the contrast between the advertisements for German winter sports and for the Utrecht Trade Fair.

And a figure in one corner: a man of about thirty, with threadbare clothes and a pallid, ill-shaven face, wearing a soft hat of some kind of grey, who looked as if he might have wandered all round Europe.

He had arrived on the train from Holland. He had shown a ticket for Bremen, and the ticket collector had explained to him in German that he had picked the most roundabout route, with no fast trains.

The man had indicated that he did not understand. He had ordered some coffee, in French, and everyone had stared at him inquisitively.

His eyes were feverish and very deep-set. He smoked with his cigarette stuck to his lower lip, a mere detail, but enough to indicate either exhaustion or contempt.

At his feet was a small fibre suitcase, the kind sold in all cheap stores. It was new.

After he'd got what he'd ordered, he fished out of his pocket a handful of loose change which included French and Belgian coins and tiny Dutch silver pieces.

The waitress had to pick out the necessary coins herself.

Less notice was taken of a passenger sitting at the next table, a tall, heavy, broad-shouldered man. He was wearing a thick black overcoat with a velvet collar, and the knot of his tie was held up by a celluloid device.

The first man seemed tense and never stopped watching the officials through the glass door, as if he were afraid of missing his train.

The second, puffing away at his pipe, studied him calmly and steadily.

The nervous passenger left his seat for a couple of minutes to go to the W.C. Then the other, without even stooping, drew the small suitcase towards him with a simple movement of his foot, and pushed an identical one into its place.

Half an hour later, the train left. The two men settled themselves in the same third-class compartment, but did not speak to each other.

At Leer, the train emptied, but continued on its way for the benefit of these two passengers.

It was ten o'clock when the train pulled in beneath the massive glass roof at Bremen, where everyone's face looked grey in the arc-lights.

*

The first passenger could not have known a word of German, because he lost his way several times, went into the first-class restaurant and, only after several comings and goings, landed up in the third-class buffet, but did not sit down at a table.

He pointed to some small rolls filled with a piece of sausage, indicated that he wished to take them away, and again paid by holding out a handful of change.

For more than half an hour he wandered through the broad streets by the station, with his small suitcase, as if he were looking for something.

The man with the velvet collar, who was following him patiently, at last understood what was on when he saw his companion plunge into a poorer district which stretched away to his left.

All he was looking for was a cheap hotel. The young man was beginning to feel tired; he looked suspiciously at a few of them before choosing a low-class establishment over the door of which was a large white frosted-glass ball.

He was still holding his suitcase in one hand and his sausage-rolls wrapped in grease-proof paper in the other.

The street was full of people. The fog was beginning to thicken, blurring the lights in the shop windows.

The man in the heavy overcoat had some difficulty getting the room next to the previous visitor.

It was a poor room, like poor rooms all over the world, with perhaps only this difference, that poverty is nowhere so depressing as in northern Germany.

But there was a communicating-door between the two rooms, and the door had a keyhole.

So the man was able to watch the suitcase being opened. All it contained was old newspapers.

The traveller went so white that it was a painful sight, and he turned the case over and over in his shaking hands, scattering the newspapers about the room.

The rolls were on the table, still in their wrapping, but the young man, who had eaten nothing since four in the afternoon, did not even glance at them.

He dashed out towards the station, losing his way and asking it a dozen times, and repeating in an accent which distorted the word so much that he was barely understood:

'*Bahnhof?* . . .'

He was in such a state that, to make himself better understood, he imitated the noise of a train!

He got to the station. He wandered about the vast departure hall, noticed a pile of luggage, and crept up to it like a thief to make sure that his case was not there.

He gave a start every time somebody passed with a suitcase of the same make.

His companion kept following him, never once letting him out of his sight.

It was midnight before they returned, one behind the other, to the hotel.

The keyhole was not big enough to show the young man slumped in his chair with his head between his hands. When he got up, he snapped his fingers in an angry yet resigned gesture.

That was the end. He took a revolver from his pocket, opened his mouth wide, and pressed the trigger.

*

A moment later, there were ten people in the room. Inspector Maigret, who had not taken off his overcoat with the velvet collar, tried to stop them going in. The words *Polizei* and *Mörder*, which means murderer, were to be heard repeatedly.

The young man was even more pathetic dead than alive. There were holes in the soles of his shoes, and his trouser-leg, which had rucked up when he fell, revealed an extraordinary red sock and a hairy, white shin.

A policeman arrived, rapped out a few orders, and everyone collected on the landing, except Maigret, who showed his Police Headquarters Inspector's badge. The policeman spoke no French, Maigret only a few stumbling words of German.

Ten minutes later, a car pulled up opposite the hotel, and some officials in civilian clothes burst in.

On the landing, the word *Franzose* had now been replaced by the word *Polizei*, and the Inspector had become an object of curiosity. But a few orders soon put a stop to the excitement, and the noise came to an end as abruptly as if someone had turned off a switch.

The visitors went back to their rooms. In the street, a silent group kept a respectful distance.

Inspector Maigret still had his pipe between his teeth, but it had gone out. His fleshy face, looking as if it had been modelled from thick clay by means of a vigorous thumb, wore a look that suggested either fear or failure.

'I must ask your permission to carry out my inquiry at the same time as yours,' he said. 'One thing is certain: this man committed suicide. He's a Frenchman.'

'Were you following him?'

'It would take too long to explain. I should like your

technical staff to take as detailed photographs as possible from all angles.'

Instead of silence, there was now excitement in the room; only two or three people were now moving about.

One of them, young and pink-faced, with a shaven head, was wearing a morning-coat and striped trousers and, from time to time, wiped the lenses of his gold-rimmed spectacles. His official title was something like *Doctor of Pathology*.

The other, equally pink, but less formally dressed, was making a thorough search, and trying hard to speak French.

They found nothing, except a passport in the name of Louis Jeunet, mechanic, born in Aubervilliers.

The revolver bore the mark of the Herstal (Belgium) arms factory.

Back at Police Headquarters, on the Quai des Orfèvres, no one suspected, that evening, that Maigret, silent, as if crushed by events, was helping his German colleagues, standing aside to make room for the photographers and police doctors, and waiting with a stubborn frown, his pipe still out, for the pathetic loot which was handed him at about three in the morning: the dead man's clothes, his passport, and a dozen photographs which the flashlights had succeeded in making strangely delusory.

He was not far, in fact he was very near believing that he had just killed a man.

Yet he did not know this man. He knew nothing about him. There was no proof that he had any accounts to settle with the law.

*

It had started the previous evening in Brussels in a most unexpected way. Maigret was there on a job. He had been conferring with the Belgian C.I.D. about some Italian refugees who had been expelled from France and whose activities were causing anxiety.

It was a job which was more like a pleasure trip. His

talks had been shorter than he had expected. The inspector had a few hours to himself.

Out of sheer curiosity, he had gone into a little café on the Montagne aux Herbes Potagères. It was ten in the morning. The café was practically deserted. But while the cheerful, friendly proprietor was chatting away to him, Maigret noticed another customer sitting at the far end of the room, in the semi-darkness, curiously employed.

The man was scruffy. He was a 'professional unemployed', the sort that exists in every capital, on the look-out for an opportunity.

He was pulling thousand-franc notes out of his pocket, counting them, wrapping them in brown paper, tying them up into a parcel, and writing an address on it.

There were at least thirty notes! Thirty thousand Belgian francs! Maigret had frowned and, when the stranger had paid for his coffee and gone out, had followed him to the nearest post office.

There, he had been able to read, over his shoulder, the address which was written in a by no means uneducated hand:

> Monsieur Louis Jeunet
> 18, rue de la Roquette
> Paris

But what struck him most was the description: *Printed Matter*.

Thirty thousand francs travelling as printed matter, like ordinary advertising hand-outs! The package was not even registered. The postal clerk weighed it, and said:

'Seventy centimes . . .'

The sender paid and went out. Maigret had noted down the name and address. He had followed his man and, for a moment, he had been amused by the chance of making the Belgian police a present. He could have gone along later to the head of the Brussels C.I.D. and said in an off-hand way:

'By the way, while I was having a glass of Gueuse-Lambic,

I ran across a crook. All you'll have to do is pick him up at such-and-such a place . . .'

Maigret was in high spirits. The town was bathed in a soft autumn sun which filled it with currents of warm air.

At eleven o'clock, the stranger bought an imitation leather, or rather imitation fibre suitcase, for thirty-two francs from a shop in the rue Neuve. Maigret, just for fun, bought a similar one, without trying to work out where it might lead him.

At half past eleven, the man entered a hotel in an alleyway, the name of which the Inspector was unable to read. He left it shortly afterwards and took the train to Amsterdam from the Gare du Nord.

This time the Inspector hesitated. Possibly the feeling that he had already seen that face somewhere influenced his decision.

'I dare say it's some trivial affair. But supposing it were something important?'

There was nothing urgent to take him back to Paris. At the Dutch frontier, he was struck by the fact that the man, with a deftness which suggested that he was used to this sort of trick, hoisted his suitcase on to the roof of the carriage before arriving at the Customs.

'We'll soon see when he stops somewhere. . . .'

But he didn't stop at Amsterdam. He merely bought a third-class ticket for Bremen. Then they crossed the flat Dutch countryside, its canals full of sailing-boats which seemed to be scudding along through the middle of the fields.

Neuschanz . . . Bremen . . .

Maigret had played his hunch and swapped over the suitcases. For hours, he had tried unsuccessfully to place the fellow in one of the categories known to the police.

'Too nervous to be a genuine international crook. Or could he be the sort of underling who gets his bosses arrested? A conspirator? An Anarchist? But he only speaks French, and there are hardly any conspirators in France, or even any active anarchists! Or a small-time crook operating on his own?'

But would a crook be living in such poverty after sending off thirty thousand francs in an ordinary brown-paper package?

The man did not drink spirits. All he did, at stations where there was a long wait, was swallow down some coffee and sometimes a roll or a *brioche*.

He did not know the line, because he kept asking for information, and worrying if he were going in the right direction, worrying unduly, in fact.

He was not strong. Yet his hands bore the marks of manual labour. His nails were black but too long, which indicated that he had not worked for some time.

His complexion suggested anaemia, maybe poverty.

Maigret had gradually forgotten the trick he was going to play on the Belgian police by bringing them a criminal bound hand and foot, as a joke.

The problem fascinated him. He kept finding excuses for himself:

'Amsterdam isn't so far from Paris. . . .'

Or:

'Bah, I can get back in thirteen hours from Bremen, by express. . . .'

*

The man was dead. He had nothing suspicious on his person, and there was nothing to indicate what he was up to except an ordinary revolver of the most common make in Europe.

He seemed to have killed himself simply because someone had stolen his suitcase. If not, why had he bought those rolls at the station buffet and not eaten them?

And why that day's journey from Brussels where he could have blown his brains out just as easily as in a German hotel?

There remained his suitcase, which might provide the

13

key to the enigma. That was why, when the body had been taken away, wrapped naked in a sheet and lifted into an official van, and after it had been examined, photographed, and studied from the soles of its feet to the crown of its head, the Inspector shut himself up in his room.

His face was drawn. Though he filled his pipe, as he always did, with little prods of his thumb, it was purely and simply to try and convince himself that he was calm.

The agonized face of the dead man preyed on his mind. He could see him again and again snapping his fingers and then straight away opening his mouth wide and firing a shot into it.

This sense of distress, almost of remorse, was so strong that he hesitated before touching the fibre suitcase.

Yet this suitcase must contain something to justify what he had done. Would he find in it evidence that the man, for whom he had been weak enough to feel sorry, was a crook or a dangerous criminal, perhaps even a murderer?

The keys were still hanging from a string tied to the handle, just as when they left the shop in the rue Neuve. Maigret lifted the lid and took out first a dark grey suit, not so worn as that of the dead man.

Under the suit were two shirts, dirty and frayed at the collars and cuffs, and rolled up into a ball.

Then a collar, with narrow pink stripes, which had been worn for at least a fortnight, because it was quite black where it had rubbed its owner's neck. Black and theadbare.

That was the lot. The bottom of the suitcase had a green paper lining, and the two straps with new buckles and tabs had not been used.

Maigret shook the clothes and went through the pockets. They were empty.

An uncertainty which he couldn't explain seized him by the throat. He went on trying to find something, because he wanted to, because he had to.

Hadn't a man killed himself because this suitcase had

14

been stolen from him? Yet all it contained was an old suit and some dirty linen.

No papers. Nothing that even resembled a document. Not even a trace of anything which bore on the dead man's past.

The room was freshly papered with cheap wallpaper, in a loud, garish flower-pattern. By contrast, the furniture was worn, wobbly, and falling to bits, and on the table there was a piece of cretonne so dirty it would have been revolting to touch.

The street was deserted. The shops had put up their shutters. But at the traffic junction, a hundred yards away, cars never stopped flowing past with a reassuring hum.

Maigret looked at the communicating-door, though he no longer dared to stoop down to the keyhole. He remembered that the experts, thinking ahead, had drawn the outline of the body on the floor of the next room.

He went in on tiptoe, so as not to waken the other visitors, but perhaps also because the mystery was weighing him down; he was still holding the crumpled suit from the suitcase.

The outline on the floor was contorted yet mathematically exact.

When he tried to fit the jacket, trousers, and waistcoat to it, his eyes lit up, and he bit the stem of his pipe without realizing.

The clothes were at least three sizes too big! They were not the dead man's!

What this tramp was so carefully preserving in his suitcase, and to which he attached such value that he killed himself because he'd lost it, was a suit belonging to somebody else!

CHAPTER 2

Monsieur Van Damme

THE Bremen papers merely carried an announcement of a few lines that a Frenchman named Louis Jeunet, a mechanic, had committed suicide in one of the town's hotels, and that his motive seemed to be poverty.

But by the time these lines appeared the next morning, the information was no longer accurate. In fact, when examining the passport, Maigret had been struck by a curious detail.

On the sixth page, for the description, where there are columns headed: *age, height, hair, forehead, eyebrows,* etc. . . . the word *forehead* came before the word *hair* instead of after it.

Now, six months earlier, the Paris C.I.D. had discovered, in Saint-Ouen, a complete factory for forged passports, army pay-books, foreign identity cards, and other official papers. A certain number of these documents had been seized, but the forgers had themselves admitted that hundreds of these forgeries from their printing-presses had been in circulation for some years and that, as they kept no books, they were unable to supply a list of their customers.

The passport proved that Louis Jeunet was one of these customers and that, consequently, his name was not Louis Jeunet.

As a result, the only more or less solid basis for an inquiry vanished. The man who had killed himself that night was no more nor less than a person unknown!

*

The authorities had given the Inspector the necessary permission, so at nine o'clock he arrived at the mortuary where the public were allowed in, once the doors were opened.

He tried unsuccessfully to find a dark corner from where he could watch, though in fact he didn't expect very much. The mortuary was a modern one, like the greater part of the city and all its public buildings.

It was more sinister even than the old mortuary in the Quai d'Horloge in Paris. More sinister for the very reason that its lines and perspective were clean, and that its uniformly white walls reflected a harsh light, and that it had cold storage units, gleaming as if in some power-station.

It suggested a model factory, a factory where the raw material was the human body.

The so-called Louis Jeunet was there, less mutilated than might have been expected, because the specialists had to some extent reconstructed his face.

There was also a young woman, and a drowned man who had been fished up in the harbour.

The attendant, glowing with health, and laced into a spotless uniform, looked more like a museum attendant.

Contrary to expectations, about thirty people filed through within an hour. When a woman asked to see a body which was not on view in the hall, electric bells rang and numbers were rapped out over the telephone.

In a section on the first floor, one of the drawers of a huge cupboard that filled an entire wall slid on to a goods-lift and, a few seconds later, a steel box appeared on the ground floor, just as books arrive in the reading-rooms of some libraries.

It was the body which had been requested! The woman leant over it, sobbed, and was led away to an office at the far end of the hall where a young clerk took down her statement.

Few people paid any attention to Louis Jeunet. However, about ten o'clock, a smartly-dressed man got out of a private car, came into the hall, looked round for the suicide and examined him closely.

Maigret was only a few steps away. He went up closer

and, looking the man over, had the impression that he was not dealing with a German.

What was more, as soon as the man saw the Inspector move, he gave a start, looked embarrassed and must have had the same impression about Maigret as the latter had had about him.

'Are you French?' he got in first.

'Yes. Are you, too?'

'In actual fact, I'm Belgian. But I've been living in Bremen for some years.'

'And do you know a man named Jeunet?'

'No! I ... I read in the paper this morning that a Frenchman had committed suicide in Bremen. I lived in Paris for a long while. I was curious and came to have a look. . . .'

Maigret was imperturbably calm, as he always was on such occasions. In fact, he looked so obstinate and unsubtle as to seem almost bovine.

'Are you from the police?'

'Yes. Police Headquarters.'

'And you came here on purpose? What am I talking about? You couldn't have, because the suicide only took place last night. Do you know some other Frenchmen in Bremen? No? If not, perhaps I can be of some help to you? May I offer an *apéritif*?'

Shortly afterwards, Maigret followed him out and got into the car which his companion was driving himself.

Words poured from the latter's mouth. He was, in fact, the typical hearty, energetic business-man. He seemed to know everyone, hailed passers-by, pointed out buildings, and explained things:

'That's the Norddeutscher Lloyd. Have you heard about the new liner they've launched? They're clients of mine.'

He pointed out a building nearly all of whose windows bore different names.

'On the fourth floor, to the left, you can see my office. . . .'

On the windows, in enamel letters, were the words: *Joseph Van Damme, Import and Export Agent*.

'Would you believe it, I sometimes go a month without having a chance to speak French? My staff and even my secretary are German. Essential – for business reasons.'

No one could have read a thought from Maigret's face. Subtlety seemed his least likely characteristic. He nodded approval. He admired what he was asked to admire, including the car. Van Damme was boasting about its patent suspension.

He accompanied him into a large *brasserie*, packed with business-men talking noisily, to the accompaniment of a tireless Viennese orchestra and the clink of beer-mugs.

'You can't imagine how many millions the customers here are worth!' Van Damme enthused. 'Listen! Do you understand German? The man next to us is selling a cargo of wool which is at this very moment *en route* from Australia to Europe. He owns thirty or forty ships. I could show you others. What will you drink? I can recommend the Pilsener. . . .

'By the way . . .'

Maigret didn't even smile at the change of subject.

'By the way, what do you make of this suicide? Was he a down-and-out, as the papers here claim?'

'It's possible. . . .'

'Are you making inquiries about him?'

'No. That's up to the German police. So, as the suicide is established . . .'

'Of course. Mind you, it only occurred to me because he was a Frenchman. So few come to the North!'

He got up to shake hands with a man who was leaving and came back hurriedly.

'You must excuse me! The director of a big insurance company. He's worth a few hundred million . . . But, look here, Inspector, it's almost midday. You will come and lunch with me, won't you? I shall have to invite you to a restaurant because I'm a bachelor. It won't be like eating in

Paris. However, I'd try and see that you didn't lunch too badly. That's settled, then, is it?'

He called the waiter over and paid. As he took his wallet from his pocket, he made a gesture which Maigret had often noticed among business-men of his kind round the Bourse, an inimitable gesture, a way of leaning backwards, sticking out the chest, drawing in the chin, and opening with casual satisfaction that sacred object, a leather case stuffed with notes.

'Let's go!'

*

It was five o'clock before he let the Inspector go, after taking him to his office where there were three clerks and a typist.

He also promised Maigret that if he did not leave Bremen that day, they would spend the evening together at a well-known cabaret.

The Inspector was once again back in the crowd, alone with his thoughts which were far from ordered. They could hardly even be described as thoughts.

In his mind, he was comparing two figures, two men, and trying to establish a link between them.

Because there *was* one! Van Damme had not gone out of his way to visit the mortuary and peer at the corpse of someone he didn't know. Nor was it merely the pleasure of speaking French that had impelled him to invite Maigret to lunch.

Besides, he had only really become natural when the Inspector appeared uninterested in the affair – or even stupid!

He had been worried that morning. His smile lacked spontaneity.

But when the Inspector had left him, he had changed and had once again become the little business-man who comes and goes, gets worked up, talks, enthuses, rubs shoulders with the big financiers, drives his car, telephones, raps out orders to his typist, gives expensive dinners, and is proud and happy to be what he is.

On the other side of the coin was a homeless, sickly-looking man in old clothes and with holes in his shoes, who had bought some sausage-rolls, never suspecting that he would not eat them.

Van Damme must have found some other companion for his evening *apéritif*, in the same atmosphere of Viennese music and beer.

At six o'clock, a metal drawer would slide noiselessly along, close on the naked body of the so-called Jeunet, and the lift would take it up to the cold storage unit where it would occupy a numbered compartment till the next day.

Maigret set off towards the Polizei Proesidium. Some policemen, stripped to the waist in spite of the time of year, were doing P.T. in a yard surrounded by bright red walls.

In the laboratory, a dreamy-eyed young man was waiting for him by a table where all the dead man's possessions were laid out and decorated with labels.

He spoke correct, academic French, and took a pride in finding the right word.

He began with the greyish suit which Jeunet was wearing when he committed suicide, explaining that the lining had been unpicked and all the seams examined, but that nothing had been found.

'The suit comes from the Belle Jardinière in Paris. The cloth is fifty per cent cotton. It is therefore a cheap garment. Grease-spots have been removed, including mineral grease which seems to indicate that the man had worked or had often been in a factory, workshop, or garage. His underclothing was unmarked. The shoes were bought in Rheims. The same goes for the suit: popular quality, mass-produced. The socks are cotton, the sort sold from stalls at four or five francs a pair. They are in holes, but have never been darned.

'All these clothes were put in a strong paper bag, shaken, and the dust collected and analysed.

'In this way, we obtained confirmation of the origin of the grease-spots. In fact, the cloth was impregnated with a fine metallic dust found only on the person of fitters, metal workers, and, in general, people who work in mechanical workshops.

'There is no such evidence in the case of the clothing which I shall call *Clothing B* and which has not been worn for several years, at least six.

'Another difference: in the pockets of *Clothing A*, we found some particles of French government tobacco, which you call "grey" tobacco.

'In the pockets of *B*, on the other hand, there was a little yellow tobacco dust, imitation Egyptian tobacco.

'But I now come to the most important point. The stains found on *Clothing B* were not grease-spots. They were old human bloodstains, probably arterial blood.

'The material has not been washed for some years. The man who was wearing the suit must have been literally drenched in blood. Finally, various tears suggest that there may have been a struggle, because in various parts, including the lapels, the weft has been ripped away as if by someone's finger-nails.

'*Clothing B* has a name-tab on it: Roger Morcel, tailor, rue Haute-Sauvenière, Liège.

'The revolver is a model which has not been manufactured for some years.

'If you would be good enough to leave me your address, I will send you a copy of the report which I have to draw up for my superiors.'

*

By eight o'clock that evening, Maigret was through with the formalities. The German police had handed over to him the dead man's clothing along with that in the suitcase, which the expert had called *Clothing B*. It had been decided that, until further orders, the body would be held at the disposal of the French authorities in the mortuary cold-storage unit.

Maigret had taken a copy of Joseph Van Damme's record: born in Liège of Flemish parents, business representative, then director of a broker's in his own name.

He was thirty-two and unmarried. He had only settled in Bremen three years before. After a difficult start, he seemed to be doing good business.

The Inspector went back to his room in the hotel, and sat for a long time on the edge of his bed, with the two fibre suitcases in front of him.

He had opened the communicating-door to the next room, where everything was still as it had been the previous day. He was struck by how little mess the incident had caused. On the wall, below a pink rose on the wallpaper, was a small brownish stain. The only bloodstain. On the table were the two sausage-rolls, still wrapped in paper. A fly had settled on them.

That morning, Maigret had sent to Paris photographs of the dead man, asking Police Headquarters to have them published in as many newspapers as possible.

Was that where the search should be made? At least the Inspector had an address in Paris: the one to which Jeunet sent himself thirty thousand-franc notes from Brussels.

Or should the search be made in Liège, where *Clothing B* had been bought some years earlier? Or in Rheims, where the dead man's shoes came from? Or in Brussels, where Jeunet had made his package of thirty thousand francs? Or in Bremen, where he had died, and where a certain Joseph Van Damme had gone and taken a quick look at his corpse, pretending he did not know him?

The hotel manager appeared and made a long speech in German, from which the Inspector gathered that he was being asked if the room where the incident had occurred could be tidied up and let again.

He grunted affirmatively, washed his hands, paid, and

went off with his two suitcases, their blatant shabbiness contrasting with his well-to-do appearance.

There was no reason why he should begin his inquiries one way rather than another. And if he settled for Paris, it was mainly because of the forcibly alien atmosphere of Germany, which constantly disrupted both his habits and way of thought, and finally had a depressing effect on him.

The tobacco, yellowish and very light, even took away his wish to smoke.

In the express, he slept, woke on the Belgian frontier at dawn, passed through Liège half an hour later and glanced half-heartedly out of the carriage window.

The train only stopped for thirty minutes, so Maigret did not have time to go to the rue Haute-Sauvenière.

At two in the afternoon, he got out at the Gare du Nord, and plunged into the Paris crowd. The first thing he did was to stop at a tobacco kiosk.

He had to hunt in his pockets a moment for some French money. Someone bumped into him. The two suitcases were at his feet. When he went to pick them up, only one was there. He looked round him in vain, realizing that it would be no good reporting it to the police.

Besides, one thing set his mind at rest. The suitcase which remained had a little string with two keys attached to the handle. It was the one which contained the clothing.

The thief had gone off with the suitcase of old newspapers.

Was it an ordinary thief, the kind that hangs round all stations? In which case, wasn't it odd that he had chosen such a shoddy-looking piece of luggage?

Maigret got into a taxi, enjoying both his pipe and the familiar hum of the street. He saw a photograph on the front page of a newspaper in a kiosk, and recognized, at a distance, the picture of Louis Jeunet, sent from Bremen.

He nearly dropped in at his house on the Boulevard Richard-Lenoir to change and to say hullo to his wife, but the incident at the station had upset him.

'If it really is *Clothing B* they're after, how can they have been told in Paris that I was bringing it or that I should be arriving at any special time?

It looked as if there were a number of mysterious circumstances attaching to the outline of that pallid face of the homeless man of Neuschanz and Bremen. Shadows were emerging, as though on a photographic plate immersed in developer.

They had to be defined, faces clarified, each one given a name; characters and entire lives reconstructed.

For the time being, there was nothing in the middle of the plate but an unclothed body, a head which the German doctors had patched up and restored to normal, and which stood out against the harsh light.

What were these shadows? First, that of a man who was running off with the suitcase that very moment, in Paris. Another who had tipped him off from Bremen or elsewhere. Perhaps it was the hearty Joseph Van Damme? Perhaps not. Then there was the person who, years earlier, had worn *Clothing B*. And the one who, in the struggle, had soaked it with his own blood. . . .

And then there was the one who had got the thirty thousand francs for the so-called Jeunet, or the one from whom the money had been stolen. . . .

The sun was shining, and people were sitting on the café terraces, which were heated by braziers. Drivers were yelling at each other. Swarms of human beings were crowding on to buses and trams.

Somewhere in that swirling crowd, and the crowds in Bremen, Brussels, Rheims, and elsewhere, two, three, four, or five persons would have to be arrested.

Perhaps more? Perhaps less. . . .

Maigret gazed affectionately at the grim façade of Police Headquarters, crossed the courtyard, holding his small suitcase, and greeted the office-boy by his Christian name.

'Did you get my telegram? Did you light the fire?'

'There's a lady here about the picture. She's been in the waiting-room two hours.'

Maigret did not bother to remove his coat and hat. He did not even put down the suitcase.

The waiting-room, at the end of the passage, with the Superintendent's offices each side of it, had frosted glass panels and was furnished with a few green velvet chairs. On the only brick wall, was a roll of police officers killed on official duty.

On one of the chairs sat a woman, still young, dressed with the typical correctness of the poor, suggesting long hours of sewing by lamplight with make-shift material.

Her black, woollen coat had a very narrow fur collar. Her hands, encased in grey cotton gloves, gripped a handbag which, like Maigret's suitcase, was of imitation leather.

Surely the Inspector must have been struck by a vague similarity between her and the dead man?

Not so much a similarity of features. But a similarity of expression, of *class* as it were.

She, too, had those same grey eyes, and the weary eyelids of one whose courage has deserted her. Her nostrils were pinched and her complexion dull.

She had been waiting for two hours and she had clearly not dared to change her seat or even move. She looked at Maigret through the glass door, not even hoping that here at last was the man she had come to see.

He opened the door.

'Would you come into my office, Madame?'

She seemed amazed when he showed her in ahead of him, and she stood for a moment, bewildered, in the middle of the room. Besides her bag, she was holding a crumpled newspaper on which could be seen half the photograph.

'I gather you know the man whose . . .'

Before he had finished speaking, she buried her face in her hands, bit her lip, and, stifling a sob, moaned:

'He's my husband, Monsieur.'

To hide his feelings, Maigret went and fetched a heavy arm-chair and pushed it towards her.

CHAPTER 3

The Herbalist's in the Rue Picpus

As soon as she could speak, she said:

'Did he suffer much?'

'No, Madame. I can assure you that death was instantaneous.'

She looked at the newspaper she was holding, and had to make an effort to speak:

'In the mouth?'

When the Inspector merely nodded, she said solemnly, and with sudden calm, staring at the floor, in the sort of tone she would have used to refer to a naughty child:

'He could never do anything the same as others!'

She did not look like anyone's mistress, or even anyone's wife. She was under thirty, yet she had the motherly tenderness, the calm gentleness of a nun.

The poor are used not to express their hopelessness, because life, work, and the hourly, daily calls of life lie for ever ahead of them. She wiped her eyes with her handkerchief. Her nose, which had become slightly red, prevented her from looking attractive.

Her lips, as she looked at the Inspector, were sometimes pursed in grief, sometimes wore a ghost of a smile.

'Do you mind if I ask you a few questions?' he said, sitting down at his desk. 'Was your husband's name really Louis Jeunet? When did he last leave you?'

She almost started crying again. Her eyes brimmed with tears. She had screwed her handkerchief into a very tight little ball between her fingers.

'Two years ago. But I saw him again once with his face pressed to the shop-window. If my mother hadn't been there . . .'

He realized that all he had to do was let her talk. She was doing it as much for her own sake as for his.

'You want to know all about our life, don't you? It's the only way to understand why Louis did this. My father was a male nurse in Beaujon. He had opened a small herbalist's in the rue Picpus, which my mother ran.

'Six years ago, my father died, and my mother and I continued to live off the business.

'I met Louis . . .'

'Did you say that was six years ago? Was he already called Jeunet?'

'Yes,' she replied in astonishment. 'He was a driller in a workshop in Belleville. He made a good living. I don't know why things happened so quickly. You can't imagine. He was impatient about everything. It was as if some fever were consuming him.

'I'd hardly been going out with him a month, when we married and he came to live with us.

'The living-quarters behind the shop are too small for three. We rented a room for my mother in the rue du Chemin-Vert. She left the business to me but, as she hadn't enough savings to live on, we used to give her two hundred francs a month.

'We were happy, I can promise you! Louis used to go off to work in the morning. My mother used to come and keep me company. He didn't go out in the evenings.

'I don't know how to explain it. But I always felt that something was wrong.

'You see, it was as if Louis wasn't our sort, as if the atmosphere got too much for him, sometimes.

'He was very loving . . .'

Her features softened. She looked almost beautiful as she confessed:

'I don't think there are many men like him. He'd take me in his arms all of a sudden. He'd gaze so hard into my eyes that it hurt. Then sometimes he'd unexpectedly push me away, in a way I've never seen anyone else do, and he'd

sigh to himself: "Still, I'm fond of you all right, Jeanne."
Then it'd all be over. He'd busy himself with one thing or
another, not even looking at me, spend hours fixing a bit
of furniture, making me a handy gadget or mending a clock.

'My mother didn't like him much, simply because she
realized he wasn't like everyone else.'

'Were there any objects among his possessions which he
kept specially carefully?'

'How did you know?'

She gave a little frightened start and said quickly:

'An old suit . . . Once, he came in when I'd taken it out
of a cardboard-box on top of the wardrobe and was brushing it. I was even going to mend the tears. The suit would
still have been good enough to wear in the house. Louis
snatched it from me, got angry and said some horrid things.
You'd have sworn he loathed me, that evening.

'It was a month after our marriage. Since when . . .'

She sighed, and looked at Maigret as if to say she was
sorry she had only such a feeble tale to tell him.

'Did he act more and more strangely?'

'It wasn't his fault, I'm sure! I think he was ill. He used
to brood. After we'd been happy for an hour in the kitchen
where we used to sit, I'd suddenly see him change. He'd
stop talking. He'd look at things and even me with an ugly
smile. Then he'd go and fling himself on his bed without
saying good night. . . .'

'Hadn't he any friends?'

'No. No one ever came to see him.'

'Didn't he travel or get any letters?'

'No. And he didn't like seeing people at home. Sometimes one of the neighbours who had no sewing-machine
used to come and have a go on mine. It was the surest way
of putting Louis in a temper.

'Not a normal sort of temper. Something deep down
inside. He was the one who seemed to be suffering.

'When I told him we were going to have a baby, he
stared at me like a madman.

'It was from then on, and especially after the baby was born, that he started to drink, in bouts, in spasms. . . .

'Yet I know he loved the baby! He used to look at him, from time to time, the way he used to look at me at first, adoringly. . . .

'The next day, he'd come back drunk, go to bed, lock the bedroom door, and spend whole hours, whole days there.

'The first few times, he cried and asked me to forgive him. Perhaps if mother hadn't interfered, I'd have managed to keep him. But my mother tried to preach to him. There were rows.

'Especially when Louis went two or three days without going to work.

'Towards the end, we were very unhappy. You know how it is, don't you? He became more and more beastly. My mother reminded him that it wasn't his house and turned him out twice.

'I'm sure it wasn't his fault. Something was driving him, driving him . . . Yet sometimes he'd look at me or his son the way I told you.

'Only it was much less often and it didn't last long. The last row was horrible. Mother was there. Louis had helped himself to some silver from the till and she called him a thief. He went quite pale, and his eyes all red, like on one of his bad days. He had a wild stare.

'I can still see him coming over to me as if he were going to strangle me. I was terrified and screamed out: "Louis!"

'He slammed the door so hard as he went out that the glass broke.

'That was two years ago. Some of the neighbours saw him pass by from time to time. I made inquiries at his factory in Belleville, but they told me he no longer worked there.

'But someone saw him in a small workshop in the rue de la Roquette which makes beer pumps.

'I saw him once after that, perhaps six months ago,

through the shop-window. Mother, who's living with me again, and the boy were in the shop. She wouldn't let me go to the door.

'Do you promise me that he didn't suffer, that he died straight away? He wasn't a happy man, you know. You must understand, now . . .'

She had lived her story through again with such intensity, and her husband moreover, had dominated her so completely that, as she talked, and she recalled his facial expressions, she unconsciously imitated them.

Maigret had been struck, from the start, by the disturbing likeness between this woman and the man in Bremen who had snapped his fingers and then fired a bullet into his mouth.

What was more, she seemed to have caught the consuming fever which she had just described. She had stopped talking, yet all her nerves were still on edge. Her breathing was shallow. She was waiting for something, she didn't know what.

'Didn't he ever talk to you about his past, his childhood?'

'No. He didn't talk much. All I know is that he was born in Aubervilliers. And I always thought he'd been educated above his station. He had lovely handwriting. He knew the Latin name for every plant. When the woman from the haberdasher's next door had a difficult letter to write, she used to come to him. . . .'

'And you never saw his family?'

'He told me, before we were married, that he was an orphan. There's something else I'd like to ask you, Inspector. Will he be brought back to France?'

When he hesitated, she turned away to hide her embarrassment and added:

'The herbalist's is my mother's now. So is the money. I know she wouldn't go to the expense of bringing back his body. Or even give me enough to go and see him. So, in that case . . .'

Her throat tightened and she hastily bent down to pick up her handkerchief, which had fallen on the floor.

'I will arrange for your husband to be brought back, Madame.'

She gave him a touching smile and dabbed at a tear on her cheek.

'You've understood, I can tell! You think like me, Inspector. It wasn't his fault. He was an unhappy man!'

'Did he ever have any large sums of money?'

'Only his pay. He used to give me it all at first. Then, when he started to drink . . .'

She gave another little smile, a very sad one, yet full of compassion.

She went away a little calmer, her narrow fur clutched tightly round her neck, still grasping her bag and the newspaper folded small in her left hand.

*

No. 18 rue de la Roquette turned out to be a really low-class hotel.

This part of the street is less than fifty yards from the Place de la Bastille. The Rue de Lappe, with its little dance-halls and its slums, leads into it.

Every ground floor is a bistro, and every house a hotel used by vagrants, permanent casual labourers, displaced persons, and prostitutes.

Yet a few workshops are squeezed into this disturbing refuge of penury, where, doors wide open, they hammer and handle oxyacetylene blow-lamps, and there is a constant flow of heavy lorries.

There is a sharp contrast between these active lives, these regular workers and busy employees with consignment notes, and the sordid, leering figures that hang about the area.

'Jeunet!' the Inspector growled, pushing open the door of the hotel office, on the mezzanine floor.

'Not here!'

'Has he still got his room?'

They had smelt the police and answered ill-humouredly.

'Yes, No. 19.'

'By the week? Or month?'

'By the month!'

'Have you any letters for him?'

They started to hedge. Finally, Maigret was handed the package Jeunet had sent himself from Brussels.

'Did he get many like this?'

'Now and then. . . .'

'Any other correspondence?'

'No. He may have got three packages altogether. A quiet fellow. I can't think why the police have got it in for him. . . .'

'Did he work?'

'At No. 65, up the road. . . .'

'Regularly?'

'It depended. Some weeks, yes. Others, no. . . .'

Maigret demanded the key of the room. But he found nothing there except a pair of unwearable shoes – the soles had come right away from the uppers – a tube which had contained aspirin and some mechanic's overalls, flung into a corner.

When he came down, he questioned the manager again, and learnt that Louis Jeunet never had any visitors, that he was never seen around with women and that, to all intents and purposes, he led a dull life, apart from occasional trips lasting three or four days.

But no one stays in a hotel in that area unless there is something funny going on. The manager knew that as well as Maigret. Eventually he grumbled:

'It's not what you think. Drink was his trouble. And how! Bouts of it. His weeklies, as my wife and I used to call them. He'd be all right for three weeks and go to work every day. Then, for a while, he'd drink away until he passed out cold on his bed. . . .'

'Wasn't there anything suspicious about him?'

But the man shrugged his shoulders as if to say that everyone who came to his establishment was suspicious.

At No. 65, they manufactured beer-pumps in a vast workshop open to the street.

Maigret was met by a foreman who had already seen Jeunet's picture in the paper.

'I was just about to write to the police,' he said. 'He was still working here last week. The fellow was earning eight francs fifty an hour!'

'When he was working.'

'You know about him? When he was working, yes! There's lots like him. But, as a rule, the others regularly have one too many or get really boozed on Saturdays. In his case, it came suddenly, without warning, a week on the trot. Once, when there was an urgent job on, I went and saw him in his room. Well, he was drinking there, all on his own, straight from a bottle on the floor by his bedside. It was no joke, I can tell you!'

*

Aubervilliers produced nothing. A Louis Jeunet, son of Gaston Jeunet, labourer, and of Berthe Marie Dufoin, domestic servant, was entered in the civil register. Gaston Jeunet had died ten years before. His wife had left the district.

Nothing was known about Louis Jeunet except that, six years before, he had written from Paris to get a copy of his birth certificate.

Yet the passport was a forgery, and therefore the man who killed himself in Bremen, and who had married the herbalist's daughter in the rue Picpus and had had a son by her, was not the real Jeunet!

The Prefecture records produced nothing either: no card in Jeunet's name, or with fingerprints corresponding to the dead man's, which had been taken in Germany.

So the wretched man had never had any account to settle with the law, either in France or abroad, because they kept up to date with the criminal records of most European countries.

It was only possible to delve back six years. This produced a Louis Jeunet, a driller, who worked, and lived the life of an honest workman.

He had married. He already owned *Clothing B* which was the cause of that first scene with his wife and which, years later, was to be the cause of his death.

He never went around with anyone and he received no letters. He seemed to know Latin, so he must have had an above-average education.

Back in his office, Maigret drew up a request for the body to the German police, dealt with a few current matters, and, with a sour, stubborn look, once again opened the yellow suitcase, the contents of which the expert in Bremen had so carefully labelled.

He added the package of thirty Belgian notes. Then he suddenly decided to break the string, copied down the numbers, and sent the list to the Brussels C.I.D., asking them to trace their origin.

He did all this laboriously, methodically, as though he were trying to convince himself that he was doing a useful job.

But from time to time he looked somewhat resentfully at the row of photographs, and his pen remained poised in the air as he gnawed at the stem of his pipe.

He was about to leave unwillingly, go home, and postpone his inquiries until the following day, when he was told that Rheims wanted him on the telephone.

It was about the picture published in the papers. The proprietor of the Café de Paris, in the rue Carnot, was convinced that he had seen the man in question in his establishment, six days before, and he remembered him because he had ultimately been forced to refuse to serve the customer, who was already drunk.

Maigret hesitated. For the second time, Rheims, where the dead man's shoes came from, was involved.

Now, these completely worn-out shoes had been bought several months earlier. Therefore, Louis Jeunet hadn't visited the town by accident.

An hour later, the Inspector took his seat in the Rheims express, and arrived there at ten o'clock in the evening. The Café de Paris, quite a smart establishment, was full of middle-class people. Three billiard-tables were in use. At several tables, cards were being played.

It was a typical French provincial café, where the customers shook hands with the cashier, and where the waiters were on familiar terms with those they served drinks. Local personalities and business representatives.

Here and there were silver-plated balls containing glass-cloths.

'I'm the Inspector you telephoned a short while ago . . .'

The proprietor was standing near the counter, keeping an eye on his staff, and at the same time handing out advice to the billiard-players.

'Ah, yes. Well, I've told you all I know. . . .'

He spoke quietly, as if he were slightly embarrassed.

'Anyway, he was sitting in that corner, near the third billiard-table, and he ordered a brandy, then a second and a third. It was about this time. The customers were giving him some funny looks because – how shall I put it? – he wasn't the sort who comes in here.'

'Had he any luggage?'

'An old suitcase, with a broken lock. I remember that, when he went out, the suitcase fell open and some old clothes dropped to the floor. He even asked for some string to tie it up.'

'Did he speak to anyone?'

The proprietor glanced at one of the billiard-players, a tall, thin, smartly-dressed fellow, who looked the sort of good player whose cannons the experts would follow with respect.

'Not exactly. Won't you have a drink? We could sit here, look!'

He chose a table to one side on which the trays were piled.

'About midnight, he was as white as this marble top. He had probably drunk eight or nine brandies. I didn't like the way he was staring. Drink does that to some people. They don't get excited, they don't wander about but, at a certain point, they fall flat on their faces. Everyone had noticed him. I went over and told him I couldn't serve him any more and he didn't object. . . .'

'Was there anyone still playing?'

'The ones you see at the third table. They're regulars who come here every evening, organize competitions, and make up a club. The man left. Then came the incident with the suitcase opening. I don't know how he was able to tie the string in the state he was in. These gentlemen shook my hand and left, and I remember one of them said: "We'll find him in the gutter somewhere!"'

The proprietor looked once more at the smartly-dressed player with the white, well-kept hands and impeccable tie, whose polished shoes creaked whenever he walked round the billiard-table.

'I don't see why I shouldn't tell you the whole story. In any case, I dare say it's just chance or a mistake. The next day, a commercial traveller, who comes here every month and who was here that evening, told me that, about one o'clock in the morning, the drunk and Monsieur Belloir were walking along side by side. He even saw the two of them go into Monsieur Belloir's house. . . .'

'He's the tall, fair man?'

'Yes. He lives five minutes away, in an attractive house in the rue de Vesle. He's the Vice-Chairman of the Banque de Crédit. . . .'

'Is the traveller here?'

'No. He's on his usual rounds, in the east. He won't be back till mid-November. I told him he must have made a mistake. But he stuck to his story. I almost mentioned it to Monsieur Belloir, as a joke. Then I didn't like to. He might have taken it badly, you see. I must ask you not to quote me on what I've just told you. Or at least, so that it doesn't seem to come from me. In my profession . . .'

The player, who had completed a break of forty-eight, looked round to take in the reactions, chalked the end of his cue with some green chalk, and, seeing Maigret with the proprietor, gave an imperceptible frown.

The latter, like most people who try to look relaxed, was wearing a worried, conspiratorial look.

'Your turn, Monsieur Émile!' Belloir called out from across the room.

CHAPTER 4

The Unexpected Visitor

THE house was a new one, and its design as well as the materials used revealed a studied elegance which created an impression of orderliness, comfort, comparative modernity, and ample means.

Red bricks, freshly repointed; stonework; a polished oak door, with brass fittings . . .

It was only half past eight in the morning when Maigret called, with the idea in the back of his mind of taking the Belloir family by surprise and seeing how they lived.

The front of the house, in any case, was worthy of the vice-chairman of a bank, and the impression was strengthened when the door was opened by a maid in a spotless apron. The entrance-hall was large and ended in a bevelled glass door. The walls were of imitation marble, and the floor of two-tone granite in geometric patterns.

To the left were double light-oak doors leading to the drawing-room and dining-room.

There was a coat-rack with some clothes on it, including an overcoat of a child of four or five, a big-bellied umbrella-stand with a gold-knobbed stick protruding from it.

The Inspector had only a second to take in the atmosphere of a solidly-organized way of living. He had hardly spoken Monsieur Belloir's name before the maid replied:

'If you would be good enough to follow me, *the gentlemen* are expecting you. . . .'

She walked towards the glass door. Through another half-opened door, the Inspector could see the dining-room, warm and clean, with a neatly laid table at which a young woman in a dressing-gown and a small boy of four were having breakfast.

Beyond the glass door was a light-coloured wooden

staircase, with a red-flowered stair carpet, secured at each step by a brass rod.

There was a large green plant on the landing. The maid was already turning the handle of another door, to a study, in which three men looked round simultaneously.

There was a sense of shock, of deep embarrassment, even of anxiety, which froze their looks. The only one who did not notice it was the maid who said in the most natural possible voice:

'Would you like to take off your coat?'

One of the three men was Belloir, neatly dressed, and his fair hair well brushed; the man next to him, less smart, was a stranger to Maigret; but the third was none other than Joseph Van Damme, the business-man from Bremen.

*

Two of them spoke at the same time. Belloir stepped forward with a frown, and said in a somewhat clipped, aloof voice which went with the *décor*:

'Monsieur?'

At the same time, Van Damme, trying to be his usual affable self, stretched out his hand to Maigret and exclaimed:

'Well, well! Fancy meeting you here. . . .'

The third man remained silent and watched the proceedings as if he had no idea what was going on.

'Excuse my disturbing you,' the Inspector began. 'I did not expect to break in on such an early meeting. . . .'

'Not at all! Not at all!' Van Damme retorted. 'Have a seat. Cigar?'

On the mahogany desk was a box. Van Damme hurried across, opened the box, and himself picked out a Havana, talking all the while.

'Wait while I find my lighter! I hope you won't summons me because it's not hall-marked! Why didn't you tell me in Bremen you knew Belloir? Just think, we could have travelled together! I left a few hours after you. I had a

40

business telegram calling me to Paris, so I took the opportunity of coming to say hullo to Belloir. . . .'

The latter remained stiff and glanced from one to the other as if hoping for some explanation. Maigret turned to him and said:

'I will keep my visit as short as possible, in view of the fact that you are expecting someone. . . .'

'I am? How did you know?'

'Simple! Your maid told me that I was expected. Now, since you couldn't have been expecting me, then obviously . . .'

His eyes were twinkling, in spite of himself, but his face was expressionless.

'Inspector Maigret, Police Headquarters. You may have seen me yesterday evening in the Café de Paris, where I was trying to get some information about a case of mine.'

'Surely it's not the Bremen affair?' said Van Damme with feigned nonchalance.

'That's precisely what it is! Would you look at this photograph, Monsieur Belloir, and tell me if it is, in fact, that of a man you brought here one night last week?'

He held out a picture of the dead man. The vice-chairman of the bank bent down but did not look at it, or at any rate did not study it.

'I don't know the fellow,' he said, handing the photograph back to Maigret.

'Are you sure it's not the man who spoke to you when you were coming back from the Café de Paris?'

'What are you talking about?'

'You must forgive me if I persist. I am trying to obtain some information which is, in any case, of only minor importance. So I have taken the liberty of disturbing you, in the belief that you would not hesitate to come to the assistance of the Law. That evening, a drunk was sitting near the third billiard-table, where you were playing. He was noticed by all the customers. He went out shortly before you and, afterwards, when you left your friends, he came up to you . . .'

'I think I remember . . . He asked me for a light.'

'And you came back here with him, didn't you?'

Belloir gave a rather disagreeable smile.

'I don't know who told you this fairy story. I am not in the habit of picking up vagrants. . . .'

'You might have recognized him as a friend, or . . .'

'I choose my friends better than that!'

'Then you returned home alone?'

'I can assure you . . .'

'Was the man the same as the one whose picture I've just shown you?'

'I don't know. I didn't even look at him. . . .'

Van Damme had been listening with obvious impatience, and several times had been on the point of interrupting. The third man, who had a small brown beard and was dressed in black clothes of a kind still fashionable among certain artists, was gazing out of the window, now and then wiping off the glass the mist caused by his breath.

'In that case, I need only thank you and apologize once again, Monsieur Belloir . . .'

'Just a minute, Inspector!' Joseph Van Damme cut in. 'Surely you're not going to leave us like that? Please stay with us a moment, and Belloir will give us some of the old liqueur brandy which he always has in reserve. You know, I was hurt that you didn't come and dine with me in Bremen. I waited for you all evening. . . .'

'Did you travel by train?'

'By air. I nearly always travel by air, like most business-men, incidentally. In Paris, I felt like saying hullo to my old friend Belloir. We were students together. . . .'

'In Liège?'

'Yes. It's nearly ten years since we saw each other. I didn't even know he was married. It's odd to find him the father of a big boy. Haven't you finished with your suicide yet?'

Belloir had rung for the maid. He told her to bring the brandy and some glasses. Every movement he made was consciously slow and precise and betrayed how worried he was underneath.

'My inquiries have only just begun,' said Maigret casually. 'I can't tell if they will take a long time or if the case will be wound up in a day or two. . . .'

The front door bell rang. The three men exchanged furtive glances. Voices could be heard on the stairs. Someone said, in a fairly strong Belgian accent:

'Are they all up there? I know the way. It's all right. . . .'

And he called out from the door:

'Hello, all!'

Dead silence greeted his words. He looked round, saw Maigret, and glanced questioningly at his companions.

'Were . . . Were you expecting me?'

Belloir's features hardened. He went up to the Inspector:

'Jef Lombard, a friend,' he said between his teeth.

Then, emphasizing every syllable, he went on:

'Inspector Maigret of Police Headquarters. . . .'

The new arrival gave a start, and stammered in a flat and slightly absurd voice:

'Oh! . . . Good. . . . Fine. . . .'

In his confusion, he handed his overcoat to the maid and then hurried after her to fetch some cigarettes from his pocket.

*

'Another Belgian, Inspector. This is a real Belgian reunion. You must think it's some sort of conspiracy. . . . How about the brandy, Belloir? A cigar, Inspector? Jef Lombard is the only one who still lives in Liège. It so happens that business has brought us all to the same place at the same time, so we've decided to celebrate the occasion with a splendid blow-out. If I might . . .'

He looked at the others with a slight hesitation.

43

'You missed the dinner I wanted to give you in Bremen. Come and have lunch with us later on. . . .'

'Unfortunately, there are some things I have to do,' Maigret replied. 'Quite apart from which, it's time I left you to your business.'

Jef Lombard had gone over to the table. He was tall, thin, and lanky, with irregular features and a pale complexion.

'Ah! Here's the photograph I was looking for,' said the Inspector, as if to himself. 'I shan't ask you if you know this man, Monsieur Lombard, because that would be too miraculous a piece of luck. . . .'

Even so, he showed him the photograph, and he saw Lombard's Adam's apple protrude even more and perform a curious up-and-down movement.

'I don't know him. . . .' he managed to get out hoarsely.

Belloir was drumming on the desk with his manicured finger-tips. Joseph Van Damme was trying to think of something to say.

'So I shan't have the pleasure of seeing you again, Inspector? Are you returning to Paris?'

'I don't know yet. . . . My apologies, gentlemen.'

Van Damme shook hands with him, so the others had to follow suit. Belloir's hand was hard and dry. The bearded fellow offered his hesitantly. Jef Lombard was busy lighting a cigarette in a corner of the study, so he merely grunted and nodded his head.

Maigret brushed past the green plant that was sticking out of a huge china vase and once more felt the stair-carpet with the brass rods under his feet. From the hall, he could hear the shrill sound of a violin being played by a beginner and a woman's voice saying:

'Not so fast. . . . Elbow level with the chin. Easy, now!'

It was Madame Belloir and her son. He could see them from the street, through the drawing-room curtains.

*

It was two o'clock, and Maigret was finishing his lunch at the Café de Paris, when he saw Van Damme come in and glance round as if he were looking for someone. The business-man smiled when he saw the Inspector, and came over to him with his hand outstretched.

'So that's what you meant by things to do!' he said. 'Lunching all by yourself in a restaurant. I quite understand. You wanted to leave us to ourselves. . . .'

He evidently belonged to that category of men who cling on to one without being asked, and refuse to see that the way one greets them is not wholly encouraging.

Maigret took a malicious pleasure in remaining very aloof, yet Van Damme sat down at his table.

'Have you finished? In that case, let me give you a liqueur. Waiter! Let's see, what will you have, Inspector? An old Armagnac?'

He had the list of special liqueurs brought, called the proprietor, finally decided on some 1867 Armagnac, and asked for balloon glasses.

'By the way. . . . Are you going back to Paris? I'm returning this afternoon and, as I loathe the train, I'm proposing to hire a car. I could take you, if you like. What do you think of my friends?'

He sniffed his Armagnac critically and drew out a cigar-case from his pocket.

'Help yourself. They are very good. There's only one place in Bremen where you can get them and they import them direct from Havana.'

Maigret's face was at its most expressionless, and his eyes completely blank.

'It's funny, meeting again after several years,' Van Damme went on, apparently unable to endure the silence. 'When you begin, at twenty, you're all level with each other, so to speak. When you meet again, it's amazing to see what a gulf has sprung up between you. I don't wish to run them down. All the same, I wasn't really at home just now at Belloir's. . . .

'That stifling provincial atmosphere. And Belloir himself, dressed up to the nines! Mind you, he hasn't done too badly. He married Morvandeau's daughter, Morvandeau the sprung-mattress man. All his brothers-in-law are in industry. And he's got quite a nice position in the bank and he'll be chairman one day or other. . . .'

'And the short man with the beard?' Maigret inquired.

'Oh, him. . . . He might do all right. I think he's a bit hard up, for the moment. He's a sculptor in Paris. Apparently, he has talent. But what can you expect? You saw him in that old-fashioned rig. Nothing modern about him. No business flair . . .'

'And Jef Lombard?'

'The grandest fellow in the world! When he was young, he was a real comedian. He'd have kept you in stitches for hours on end. . . .

'He wanted to be a painter. To earn a living, he drew for the newspapers. Then he worked as a photo-engraver, in Liège. He's married. I think his third's on the way. . . .

'What I mean is that I feel as if I'm suffocating when I'm with them. Petty lives and petty worries. It's not their fault, but I can't wait to get back to my business atmosphere. . . .'

He emptied his glass, and looked round the almost deserted room where a waiter was sitting at a table on the far side, reading the newspaper.

'That's agreed, then? You'll come back to Paris with me?'

'But aren't you taking the small man with the beard who came with you?'

'Janin? No! He'll have caught the train by now. . . .'

'Is he married?'

'Not exactly. But he always has some girl-friend or other living with him, sometimes for a week, sometimes even a year. Then he has a change! But he always introduces his female companion to you as Madame Janin. . . . Waiter! The same again!'

Maigret had to take care at times not to let his eye become too piercing. The proprietor himself came over and told him that he was wanted on the telephone. He had left the address of the Café de Paris at the Quai des Orfèvres.

It was some news from Brussels which had been wired to Police Headquarters. *The thirty thousand-franc notes had been issued by the Banque Générale de Belgique to a certain Louis Jeunet in payment of a cheque signed Maurice Belloir.*

When he opened the door of the telephone-box, Maigret noticed that Van Damme, not realizing he was being watched, had let his face relax. He immediately seemed less chubby, less pink, and, above all, less bursting with health and optimism.

He must have sensed that someone was looking at him, because he gave a start, and automatically became the hearty business-man again.

'That's agreed, then?' he said. 'You'll come with me? *Patron!* Will you arrange for us to be picked up by car and driven to Paris? A comfortable car, you understand? And while we're waiting, the same again. . . .'

He chewed the end of his cigar and, for a split second, as he was staring at the marble table-top, his eyes dulled and the corners of his mouth drooped as if the tobacco was too bitter for him.

'It's when you live abroad that you really appreciate French wines and liqueurs!'

The words rang hollow. There was clearly a deep gulf between them and the thoughts that were passing through his head.

Jef Lombard passed in the street. His figure was slightly blurred by the net curtains. He was alone. He was taking long, slow, gloomy strides and not bothering to look at what was going on in the town.

He was carrying a travelling-bag which reminded Maigret of the two yellow suitcases. But it was a better quality one, with two straps and a pocket for a visiting-card.

The heels of his shoes were beginning to wear down on

47

one side. His clothes were clearly not brushed every day. Jef Lombard was making for the station on foot.

Van Damme, a large platinum signet-ring on one finger, was wreathed in a cloud of fragrant smoke, spiced with the sharp tang of alcohol. The proprietor could be heard muttering over the telephone to the garage.

Belloir would be leaving his new house on his way to the marble entrance of the bank, while his wife took their son for a walk up and down the avenues.

Everyone would say good morning to him. His father-in-law was the biggest business-man in the area. His brothers-in-law were in industry. He had fine prospects.

Janin, with his black goatee and flowing cravat, would be on his way to Paris – third-class, Maigret would have betted.

Right at the bottom of the scale was the white-faced passenger from Neuschanz and Bremen, the husband of the herbalist in the rue Picpus, the driller from the rue de la Roquette, the solitary drinker, who used to stare at his wife through the shop-window, who sent himself banknotes wrapped like old newspapers, who bought sausage-rolls in a station buffet, and shot himself in the mouth because an old suit which was not his had been stolen from him.

'Are you ready, Inspector?'

Maigret gave a start and stared vaguely at his companion, so vaguely that the latter was embarrassed, tried to laugh – feebly! – and stammered:

'Were you dreaming? In any case, you seemed miles away. I bet you're still worrying about your suicide. . . .'

Not altogether. Because, just as he was asked this question, Maigret, without knowing why himself, was making up a strange list; the number of children involved in the story: one in the rue Picpus, with his mother and grandmother, in a shop smelling of mint and rubber; one in Rheims, learning to keep his elbow level with his chin, and drawing a bow across the strings of a violin; two in Liège, at Jef Lombard's, and a third on the way. . . .

'A last Armagnac. What do you say?'

'No thank you. That's enough. . . .'

'Come along! The stirrup-cup, one for the road. . . .'

Joseph Van Damme was the only one to laugh; he constantly felt the need, like a small boy who is afraid to go down into the cellar and who whistles to convince himself that he is brave.

CHAPTER 5

Breakdown at Luzancy

As they drove at high speed through the gathering dusk, there was rarely a moment's silence. Joseph Van Damme constantly found something to talk about and, with the help of the Armagnac, managed to keep up his high spirits.

The car was an old private saloon with worn cushions, flower-vases and marquetry pockets. The chauffeur was wearing a trench coat, and a knitted scarf round his neck.

After they had been driving for nearly two hours, they slowed down, and the car stopped by the side of the road about a mile from a village, the lights of which were just visible through the mist.

The chauffeur leant over the rear wheels, opened the door, and said that they had a puncture, and that it would take about a quarter of an hour to fix it.

The two men got out. The driver was already putting a jack under the axle, assuring them that he did not need any help.

Was it Maigret or Van Damme who suggested a stroll? In fact, neither did. It came about naturally. They took a few steps down the road, and noticed a narrow path at the end of which was a fast-flowing river.

'Look! The Marne,' said Van Damme. 'It's in flood.'

They followed the path slowly, smoking their cigars. They could hear an indistinct sound, and only found out where it came from when they reached the bank.

A hundred yards away, on the far side of the water, was a lock, Luzancy lock, its approaches deserted and its gates shut. Below the two men was the weir, with its creamy falls, its swirls and eddies, and its powerful current. The Marne was swollen.

In the darkness, they could make out the branches of

trees, even whole tree-trunks swept along by the current, crashing into the weir and finally shooting it.

There was only one light: the one on the lock in front of them.

At that very moment, Joseph Van Damme was in the middle of his speech, and saying:

'. . . Every year the Germans are making fantastic efforts to harness energy from rivers, and the Russians are copying them. They're building a dam in the Ukraine which will cost a hundred and twenty million dollars, and which will supply electric power to three provinces. . . .'

It was barely perceptible: his voice faltered on the words *electric power*. Then it went on as confidently as before. Then the man seemed to have to cough, and to take his handkerchief out of his pocket and wipe his nose.

They were less than eighteen inches from the water and suddenly Maigret, pushed from behind, lost his balance, swayed, and fell forwards. He clung with both hands to the grass on the bank; his feet were in the water, and his hat went floating over the weir.

Things happened quickly. The Inspector had been expecting that push. Some clods of earth gave way under his right hand.

But he had noticed a branch with some give, so he grasped it with his left.

It was barely a few seconds before he was on his knees on the towpath, then on his feet, and yelling at a figure vanishing into the distance:

'Stop!'

The odd thing was that Van Damme seemed afraid to run. He was making for the car, but hardly seemed to be hurrying. His knees were weak with fear and he kept looking round.

Head down and his neck buried in the collar of his overcoat, he let Maigret catch him up. He made only one gesture, a gesture of fury, as if he were thumping an imaginary table, and muttered between his teeth:

'Idiot!'

To be on the safe side, Maigret had pulled out his revolver. Without letting go of it, and without taking his eyes off his companion, he shook his trousers which were soaked to the knees. The water squelched from his shoes.

The chauffeur gave a few little hoots from the road to tell them that the car was ready to go again.

'Come on!' said the Inspector.

They went back to their seats in silence. Van Damme still had his cigar between his teeth. He avoided Maigret's eyes.

Ten miles. Twenty miles. A built-up area through which they slowed down; people wandering about the lighted streets. Then the main road again.

'Anyway, you can't arrest me. . . .'

The Inspector gave a start. The words, uttered slowly and stubbornly, were so unexpected. Yet they perfectly expressed what he was thinking.

They reached Meaux. The country gave place to the outer suburbs. A fine drizzle began to fall and, each time they passed a street-lamp, every drop became a star.

Then the Inspector, his mouth to the speaking-tube, said:

'Drive us to Police Headquarters, Quai des Orfèvres. . . .'

He filled his pipe. He could not light it because his matches were damp. He could not see his neighbour's face, which was turned towards the door, and which was now a mere profile, blurred by the shadows. But he could sense the anger in it.

There was now something hard, bitter, and intense in the atmosphere.

Even Maigret was sticking his lower jaw out grimly.

The tension was illustrated by an absurd incident, when the car stopped outside Police Headquarters. The Inspector got out first.

'Come on!' he said.

The chauffeur was waiting to be paid and Van Damme

did not appear to be doing anything about it. There was a moment of indecision. Then, Maigret, not unaware of the absurdity of the situation, said:

'Well? You hired the car. . . .'

'Excuse me. I travelled as a prisoner, so it's up to you to pay. . . .'

It was this detail which betrayed how far they had progressed since leaving Rheims, and the change that had come over the Belgian.

Maigret paid and, without a word, showed his companion the way. Closing the door of his office, the first thing he did was make up the stove.

He opened a cupboard, took out some clothes, and, ignoring his visitor, changed his trousers, socks, and shoes, and put his wet things to dry by the fire.

Van Damme had sat down without being asked. In the bright light, the change was even more striking.

He had left his false bonhomie, his out-spokenness and his somewhat forced smile behind in Luzancy, and he was waiting, his features drawn and a furtive look on his face.

Maigret kept busying himself about the room and pretending to ignore him, arranging his files and telephoning to his chief to ask him about something which had nothing to do with the case in hand.

Finally, planting himself in front of Van Damme, he said:

'Where, when, and how did you come to know the Bremen suicide who was travelling with a passport in the name of Louis Jeunet?'

The other gave an imperceptible start. But he glanced up with a determined look and said:

'In what capacity am I here?'

'Do you refuse to answer my question?'

Van Damme gave a laugh, a new kind of laugh, ironical and unpleasant.

'I know the law quite as well as you do, Inspector.

Either you are charging me and I shall wait until I see the warrant for my arrest, or else you are not charging me and I do not have to answer.

'In the first case, the law states that I may wait legal aid before speaking.'

Maigret did not get annoyed. He did not even seem put out by this attitude. Quite the contrary. He looked at his companion inquisitively, almost with satisfaction.

Thanks to the incident in Luzancy, Joseph Van Damme had been obliged to drop any pose. Not only the one he adopted with Maigret, but with everyone else, even himself.

Barely a trace remained of the hearty, superficial Bremen business-man, going from the big cafés to his modern office and from his office to the well-known restaurants. Nothing remained of the light-hearted, breezy commercial agent tackling his work and piling up money with the cheerful energy and zest of a man who enjoys life.

All that remained was a face, as though carved in wood, drained of colour, and it almost seemed as if, in the space of an hour, bags had formed under the eyes.

Yet, an hour earlier, Van Damme had still been a free man who, though he had something on his conscience, retained the self-assurance given him by his reputation, money, ability, and cunning.

He noticed the difference himself.

In Rheims, he used to pay for round after round of drinks. He would offer his companions the best cigars. He would give his orders and the proprietor would do his best to please him, telephone the garage and advise them to send their most comfortable car.

He was *someone*!

In Paris, he had refused to pay for the ride. He invoked the law. He seemed ready to argue, to defend himself inch by inch, dourly, like a man fighting for his life.

He was furious with himself. What he had said, after his gesture by the bank of the Marne, proved it.

He had planned nothing in advance. He did not know the

chauffeur. Even at the time of the breakdown, he had not immediately realized how he could make use of it.

It was only at the water's edge. Those swirls and eddies. The trees floating by as if they were dead leaves.

Stupidly, without thinking, he had given that push with his shoulder. . . .

He was furious. He guessed that his companion had been expecting that move.

He probably even realized that the game was up, and therefore he was all the more determined to fight back desperately.

He made as if to light another cigar. Maigret took it from his mouth, flung it into the coal-scuttle, and then went on and removed the hat which Van Damme had kept on his head.

*

'I must warn you that I have my work to do. If you do not propose to arrest me in accordance with official regulations, I must ask you to be good enough to release me. If you do not, I shall be forced to bring an action for arbitrary arrest.

'I may as well tell you that I shall strenuously deny any hand in the soaking you received. You stumbled on the slippery mud on the towpath. The chauffeur will confirm that I didn't try to run away, as I should have if I had really tried to drown you.

'As for the rest, I am still waiting to know what you have against me. I came to Paris on business. I can prove it. Then I went to Rheims to see an old friend, as highly-considered as myself.

'I was foolish enough, meeting you in Bremen where there are very few Frenchmen, to make a friend of you, take you out to eat and drink, and finally give you a lift back to Paris.

'You showed my friends and myself the photograph of a man we do not know. He killed himself. This has been materially proved. No one has brought an action so consequently there are no judicial steps to be taken.

'That is all I have to say to you. . . .'

Maigret pushed a spill into the stove, lit his pipe, and merely said:

'You are quite free. . . .'

He could not help smiling, because Van Damme was thrown right off balance by so easy a victory.

'What do you mean?'

'You're free! That's all. I may add that I am prepared to return your kindness and invite you to dinner. . . .'

He had seldom been in such high spirits. The other stared at him in astonishment verging on terror, as if each of his words was charged with hidden menace. He got up hesitantly.

'Am I free to return to Bremen?'

'Why not? You have just told me yourself that you are not guilty of any offence. . . .'

For a moment, it seemed that Van Damme was about to recover his self-assurance and cheerfulness, even accept the invitation to dinner, and explain away his action in Luzancy as clumsiness or a rush of blood to the head.

But Maigret's smile quenched this flicker of optimism. He seized his hat and clapped it on his head.

'What do I owe you for the car?'

'Nothing whatever. Only too glad to have been of service. . . .'

Were the man's lips trembling? He did not know how to take his leave. He tried to find something to say. Finally, he shrugged and made for the door, muttering, though it would have been hard to tell quite to whom or what the expression referred:

'Fool!'

Out on the staircase, where the Inspector was leaning over the banisters, watching him go, he repeated the same word.

Sergeant Lucas was passing with a handful of files, on his way to his boss's office.

'Quick! Get your hat . . . And coat. Follow that man to the end of the earth, if necessary. . . .'

Maigret took the files from his subordinate.

*

The Inspector had just completed a certain number of questionnaires, each headed by a name, to be sent out to the various divisions and returned to him with detailed information about the persons involved, namely: Maurice Belloir, vice-chairman of a bank, rue de Vesle, Rheims; Jef Lombard, photo-engraver, Liège; Gaston Janin, sculptor, rue Lepic, Paris; and Joseph Van Damme, import–export agent, Bremen.

He had reached the last card when the office-boy came and told him that a man wanted to see him in connexion with Louis Jeunet's suicide.

It was late. Police Headquarters was almost deserted. In the next office, though, an inspector was typing a report.

'Send him in!'

The person who was shown in stopped at the door, with an awkward, worried look. Maybe he was already regretting what he had done.

'Come in. Have a seat.'

Maigret took stock of him. He was tall and thin, with very fair hair, ill-shaven, and had on shabby clothes not unlike Louis Jeunet's. His overcoat had a button missing; its collar was greasy and its lapels unbrushed.

From other little details, his manner, and the way he sat down and looked about him, the Inspector summed him up as a casual worker, who, even if on the right side of the law, could not disguise his anxiety when confronted with the police.

'Have you come because of the picture that appeared in the newspapers? Why didn't you report straight away? The photograph has been out two days. . . .'

'I don't read the newspapers,' the man began. 'My wife

happened to bring back a piece of one wrapped round her shopping.'

Once before Maigret had been struck by these same mobile features, constantly twitching nostrils and, above all, this worried, morbidly worried look.

'Do you know Louis Jeunet?'

'I can't tell. It's a bad photograph. But I think . . . I think it's my brother. . . .'

Maigret let slip a sigh of relief. He felt that, this time, the mystery would be cleared up straight away. He went and planted himself with his back to the stove, the way he usually stood when he was in a good mood.

'In that case, your name must be Jeunet?'

'No. That's just it. That's why I hesitated to come. Yet it's definitely my brother. I'm sure of it, now I've seen a better photo on your desk. That scar, for instance! But I can't understand why he killed himself and, what's more, why he changed his name. . . .'

'What's yours?'

'Armand Lecocq d'Arneville. I've brought my papers.'

That movement, too, towards his pocket to take out his grimy passport, betrayed him as a casual worker, used to being under suspicion and having to show his identification papers.

'D'Arneville with a small d? In two words?'

'Yes.'

'You were born in Liège,' the Inspector continued, glancing at the passport. 'You are thirty-five. What is your profession?'

'At the moment, I'm a messenger in a factory in Issy-les-Moulineaux. My wife and I live in Grenelle.'

'You're down here as a mechanic.'

'I was once. I've done a bit of everything.'

'Including time. . . .' Maigret observed, turning over the pages of the passport. 'You're a deserter. . . .'

'There was an amnesty. I can explain. My father had money. He ran a tyre-business. I was only six when he left my mother. She'd just had my brother Jean. That's how it all started. . . .

'We settled down in a small place in the rue de la Province, in Liège. In the early days, my father used to send us money for our upkeep fairly regularly.

'He led a gay life. He had mistresses. Once, when he brought us our monthly allowance, there was a woman in the car waiting down below. . . .

'There were rows. My father stopped paying, or at least only sent instalments. My mother used to go out cleaning and she gradually became half-mad.

'Not mad enough to be put away. But she used to accost people and tell them her troubles. She would wander round the streets, crying. . . .

'I hardly saw my brother. I used to go about with the local kids. We were carted off a dozen times to the police station. Then I was sent to work in an ironmonger's.

'I went home as little as possible. My mother was always crying, and she used to collect the old women in the neighbourhood and moan with them.

'When I was sixteen, I enlisted in the army, and applied to be sent to the Congo. I only stayed there a month. I hid in Matadi for a week. Then I stowed away on a passenger-ship bound for Europe.

'I was caught. I did time. I escaped and came to France and did all sorts of jobs.

'I've starved. I've slept in the Halles. I haven't always been perfect, but I swear that for the last four years I've been going steady.

'I've even got married. To a factory-girl who's keeping on with her job, because I don't earn much and I'm sometimes out of work.

'I've never tried to go back to Belgium. Someone told me that my mother died in a lunatic asylum and that my father was still alive.

'But he never wanted to know us. He's got another family. . . .'

The man gave a half-smile, as if to excuse himself.

'What about your brother?'

'That's different. Jean was the steady sort. He won a scholarship and went on to college. When I left Belgium for the Congo, he was only thirteen and I haven't seen him since.

'I sometimes had news when I ran into people from Liège. After college, some people helped him to study at the University.

'That was ten years ago. After that, all the Belgians I met told me they knew nothing about him, and that he must have gone abroad, because they never heard him mentioned.

'It was a shock to see the photograph, and especially to think that he'd died in Bremen, under a false name.

'You can't understand. I started off on the wrong foot. I've failed. I've been stupid.

'But when I think of Jean at thirteen . . . He was like me, but calmer, more serious. He used to read poetry, even then. He used to spend nights at his books, all alone, by the light of some stumps of candle a sacristan gave him.

'I was sure he'd make good. Look, as a small boy, he wouldn't have run round the streets for all the tea in China. In fact, the local bad boys used to jeer at him.

'I've always needed money, and I didn't hesitate to ask my mother. She went short so as to give it to me. She worshipped us. You don't understand when you're sixteen. But I remember I was horrible to her one day, because I'd promised to take a girl to the cinema.

'My mother was broke. I cried and threatened her. A charity organization had just given her some medicines so she went and sold them back.

'Do you understand? And now it's Jean who's dead, just like that, up there, under another name.

'I don't know what he's done. I can't believe he's gone the same way as me. You'd think the same if you'd known him as a boy.

'Do you know anything?'

Maigret handed him back his passport.

'Do you know any Belloirs, Van Dammes, Janins, and Lombards in Liège?'

'A Belloir, yes. His father was a local doctor. The son was a student. But they were "posh" people. I had nothing to do with them. . . .'

'What about the others?'

'I've heard the name Van Damme before. I think there used to be a big grocer's in the rue de la Cathédrale with that name. But it's so long ago.'

Then, after a moment's hesitation, Armand Lecocq d'Arneville added:

'Could I see Jean's body? Has it been brought back?'

'It will be in Paris tomorrow.'

'Are you quite sure he killed himself?'

Maigret looked away, embarrassed by the thought from which he could see no escape, that he had been involved in the incident and had been the unconscious cause of it.

His companion was screwing up his cap and shifting from one foot to another, waiting to be sent away. His deep-set eyes, and his pupils lost, like grey confetti, behind their pale eyelids, recalled so vividly the meek, worried eyes of the passenger from Neuschanz that Maigret felt a painful stab of remorse.

CHAPTER 6

The Hanged Men

It was nine o'clock in the evening. Maigret was at home in the Boulevard Richard-Lenoir, without his collar or coat, and his wife was busy sewing, when Lucas came in drenched, brushing the rain, which had been coming down in bucketfuls, from his shoulders.

'The man's gone,' he said. 'So, as I didn't know if I ought to follow him abroad . . .'

'To Liège?'

'That's right! Did you already know? His luggage was at the Hôtel du Louvre. He had dinner there, changed and took the 6.19 p.m. for Liège. First-class single ticket. He bought a whole pile of magazines at the station bookstall. . . .'

'You'd think he gets under my feet on purpose!' the Inspector growled. 'In Bremen, when I didn't even know he exists, he introduces himself to me at the mortuary, asks me out to dinner and clings on to me. I arrive in Paris. He's here a few hours before or after me. Probably before, because he travelled by air. I go to Rheims and there he is ahead of me. I decide, an hour ago, to go to Liège tomorrow, and he's been there since this evening! To crown it all, he knows quite well that I'm going to turn up and that his merely being there practically constitutes a charge against him. . . .'

Lucas, who knew nothing about the case, suggested:

'Perhaps he wants to draw suspicion on himself so as to save someone else?'

'Is it to do with a crime?' Madame Maigret asked quietly, still sewing away.

Her husband got up with a sigh and gazed at the arm-chair where he had been so comfortably seated a moment earlier.

'What time is there still a train for Belgium?'

'There's only the night train now, at 9.30 p.m. It gets into Liège about six in the morning.'

'Will you pack my suitcase?' the Inspector said to his wife. 'How about a drink, Lucas? Help yourself. You know the cupboard. I've just got some of the plum brandy my sister-in-law makes herself, in Alsace. It's the long-necked bottle. . . .'

He dressed, removed *Clothing B* from the yellow fibre suitcase, wrapped it up well, and put it into his travelling-bag. Half an hour later, he left, accompanied by Lucas, who asked him while they were waiting for a taxi:

'What is this case? I haven't heard it mentioned back at H.Q.'

'I don't know much more about it myself,' the Inspector admitted. 'This odd sort of fellow died, right in front of me, idiotically, and there's a hell of a mix-up over what he did which I'm trying to sort out. I've been rushing at it like a wild boar, and I wouldn't be surprised if I didn't get my knuckles rapped for my pains. Here's a taxi! Shall I drop you in town?'

*

It was eight in the morning when he left the Hôtel du Chemin de Fer, facing the Guillemins station, in Liège. He had bathed and shaved; under his arm he was carrying a parcel containing not the whole of *Clothing B*, but only the coat. He found the rue Haute-Sauvenière, a steep, very busy street, and asked for Morcel's, the tailor. It was a poorly lit house, and a man in shirt-sleeves took the coat and turned it over and over in his hands, asking questions:

'It's a very old thing,' he declared, after considering it. 'It's torn. There's nothing to be done with it. . . .'

'It doesn't convey anything to you?'

'Nothing at all. The collar's badly cut. It's imitation English cloth, made in Verviers.'

The man began to chatter.

63

'Are you French? Does this coat belong to someone you know?'

Maigret sighed and took back the coat, while the other man kept talking, ending up where he should have started:

'You understand, I've only been here six months. If I'd made that suit, it wouldn't have had time to wear out. . . .'

'What about Monsieur Morcel?'

'He's at Robermont!'

'Is it far from here?'

The tailor laughed, delighted at his mistake, and explained:

'Robermont's the cemetery. Monsieur Morcel died at the beginning of the year and I took over the business. . . .'

Maigret found himself out in the street, with his parcel under his arm. He reached the rue Hors-Château, one of the oldest in the town where, at the far side of a courtyard, a zinc plaque bore the inscription: *Central Photo-engraving – Jef Lombard – Rapid work of all kinds.*

The Old Liège-style windows had small panes. In the middle of the small unevenly paved courtyard was a fountain carved with some former nobleman's arms.

The Inspector rang. He heard footsteps coming down from the first floor, and an old woman half-opened up and pointed to a glass door.

'All you have to do is push it. The workshop's at the end of the passage.'

It was a long room, lit by a glass roof. Two men in blue overalls were moving about among the zinc plates and trayfuls of acid. The floor was strewn with photographic proofs, and paper blotched with printer's ink.

The walls were covered with advertisements. Covers of magazines had been stuck on them, too.

'Monsieur Lombard?'

'He's in the office, with a gentleman. This way. Mind you don't get dirty. Turn to the left. It's the first door.'

The place must have been built bit by bit. You went up and down steps. Doors led into unused rooms.

It was both old-fashioned and oddly cheerful, like the old woman who'd been the first to see Maigret, and the workmen.

Arriving in an ill-lit passage, the Inspector heard voices, thought he recognized Joseph Van Damme's, and tried to listen. But they were too indistinct. He took a few more steps and the voices stopped. A head was poked through the half-open door. It was Jef Lombard's.

'Is it for me?' he called, not recognizing his visitor in the semi-darkness.

The office was a smaller room than the others, furnished with a table, two chairs, and shelves full of photographic plates. On the untidy table were bills, prospectuses, and headed notepaper from various business firms.

Van Damme was there, sitting on the corner of the desk. After a vague nod to Maigret, he made no move, and looked straight in front of him, scowling.

Jef Lombard was in working-clothes, his hands were dirty, and he had little black spots on his face.

'Can I help you?'

He cleared a chair covered with papers, pushed it over to the visitor, and hunted for the cigarette-end which he had put on a shelf. It was starting to burn the wood.

'Just a little information,' said the Inspector, without sitting down. 'I'm sorry to disturb you. I would like to know if, a few years ago, you knew a certain Jean Lecocq d'Arneville. . . .'

It was as if he'd pressed a trigger. Van Damme gave a start but took care not to turn towards Maigret. The photo-engraver bent down hastily to pick up a crumpled paper lying on the floor.

'I have . . . I think I have heard that name before,' he muttered. 'He's from Liège, isn't he?'

He had gone pale. He shifted a pile of photographic plates.

'I don't know what became of him . . . It . . . It's so long ago. . . .'

'Jef! Quick, Jef!'

It was a woman's voice from the maze of passages. A woman came running, out of breath, and stopped in front of the open door, so excited that her legs were trembling. She was moppping her brow with a corner of her apron. Maigret recognized the old woman who had let him in.

'Jef!'

Pale with emotion, eyes shining, he answered:

'What is it?'

'A girl! Quick!'

He looked round him, stammered something indistinct, and shot out of the door.

*

The two men were left alone. Van Damme took a cigar from his pocket, lit it slowly, and trod out the match. His face was hard, as at Police Headquarters. His mouth drooped and his jaws twitched as before.

But the Inspector pretended to take no notice of him and, hands in his pockets and pipe between his teeth, he began to wander round the office and examine the walls.

Only a few inches of wall were visible here and there because, wherever there were no shelves, drawings, water-colours, and paintings had been pinned up.

The paintings were not framed. They were simply canvases on stretchers, rather clumsy landscapes, with the grass and the leaves of the trees in the same thick green.

There were also a few caricatures, signed *Jef*, sometimes touched up with water-colour, sometimes cut out of a local paper.

But what struck Maigret was the large number of drawings of another kind, variations on the same theme. The paper had yellowed. A few dates helped to place the period when these sketches had been made as about a dozen years before.

They were differently composed, infinitely more romantic and, in ways, suggested a student imitating the style of Gustave Doré.

An early ink-sketch represented a hanged man swinging from a gibbet on which was perched an enormous crow. Hanging was the theme of at least thirty of these bits of work, either in pencil, ink, or water-colour.

There was the edge of a forest, with a man hanging from the branch of every tree. Somewhere else was a church steeple, and a human body hanging from both arms of a cross below the weather-cock.

There were hanged men of every kind. Some were dressed in sixteenth-century costume, forming a kind of Court of Miracles where everyone was swinging a few feet above the ground.

There was a hanged lunatic, in a top-hat and tail-coat, holding a stick, whose gibbet was a lamp-post.

Below another sketch was some writing: four lines from Villon's *Ballade des Pendus*.

There were dates, too, always the same period. All these macabre drawings, done ten years earlier, were now rubbing shoulders with captioned sketches for humorous newspapers, drawings for calendars, landscapes of the Ardennes, and advertising posters.

The steeple theme recurred, too. And the whole church. From the front, from the side, and from below. The main door, on its own. The gargoyles. The forecourt, with its six steps, which the perspective made seem vast.

Always the same church. As Maigret passed from wall to wall, he felt that Van Damme was growing agitated and ill at ease, perhaps even a prey to the same temptation as at Luzancy weir.

A quarter of an hour went by this way, and then Jef Lombard returned, his eyes moist. He wiped his forehead across which a lock of hair was straggling.

'You must forgive me,' he said. 'My wife has just given birth. To a girl. . . .'

There was a hint of pride in his voice but, as he spoke, he glanced anxiously from Maigret to Van Damme.

'It's my third child. Yet I'm just as overcome as the first

time. You saw my mother-in-law. She had eleven and yet she's sobbing for joy. She went and shouted the good news to the workmen and wanted to take them to see the baby. . . .'

His eyes followed Maigret's and came to rest on the steeple with the two hanged men. He became more nervous, and murmured with obvious embarrassment:

'Youthful indiscretions. They're very bad. But at the time I thought I'd be a great artist. . . .'

'It is a church in Liège?'

Jef did not answer immediately. Finally, he said, almost regretfully:

'It's been gone for seven years. It was demolished to build a new church. It wasn't beautiful. It hadn't even any style. But it was very old, with something mysterious about its design and the alleyways which surrounded it and which have since been cleared away. . . .'

'What was its name?'

'The church of Saint-Pholien. The new one, built on the same site, has the same name.'

Joseph Van Damme was fidgeting as if his nerves were raw. Underneath, he was ill at ease, though it showed only in scarcely perceptible movements, in his irregular breathing, his trembling fingers, and his leg which was pressed up against the desk, but which kept swinging.

'Were you married at the time?' Maigret inquired.

Lombard laughed.

'I was nineteen. I was studying at the Academy. Look!'

He pointed with a look of nostalgia, at a bad portrait, in dreary colours, where he was, however, still recognizable, thanks to the characteristic irregularity of his features. His hair was growing down his neck. He was wearing a black tunic, buttoned up to the neck, and a flowing cravat.

The picture was extravagantly romantic and there was even the traditional skull in the background.

'Just imagine if you'd told me then I was to be a photo-engraver!' said Jef Lombard ironically.

He seemed as embarrassed by Van Damme's presence as by Maigret's. But he obviously did not know how to get rid of them.

A workman came and asked him about a plate that was not ready.

'They can come back this afternoon!'

'Apparently that'll be too late!'

'Who cares? Tell them I've got a daughter. . . .'

His eyes, his gestures, and the pallor of his complexion, dotted with little spots of acid, betrayed a confused mixture of joy, nervousness, and anxiety.

'Will you have something? We'll go into the house.'

All three walked along the maze of passages and through the door which the old woman had opened to Maigret earlier.

There were blue tiles in the passage. The place smelt clean, though there was a mawkish air about, possibly from the stuffiness of the sickroom.

'The two boys are at my brother's. This way.'

He opened the dining-room door. Only a glimmer of daylight filtered through the small window-panes. The furniture was gloomy, though the brass on show round the room reflected the light.

On the wall was a large portrait of a woman, signed *Jef*, clumsily painted, but clearly showing that he had tried to idealize his model.

Maigret took it to be his wife, looked around and, as he expected, found more hanged men. Better ones. Some that were thought worth framing.

'Will you have a glass of gin?'

The Inspector felt Joseph Van Damme's angry gaze on him. Every detail of the conversation seemed to infuriate him.

'You said just now that you knew Jean Lecocq d'Arneville. . . .'

Footsteps could be heard from the floor above, presumably the room in which the woman had had her baby.

'A casual acquaintance. . . .' Jef Lombard replied distractedly, straining to catch a low sound of wailing.

He raised his glass and said:

'To my daughter's health! And my wife's!'

He turned sharply, drained his glass at one gulp, and went and looked for some non-existent object in the sideboard to hide his confusion; but the Inspector still caught the dull sound of a stifled sob.

'I must go upstairs. Forgive me. . . . One of those days. . . .'

*

Van Damme and Maigret had not exchanged a word. While they were crossing the yard and skirting the well, the Inspector studied his companion ironically, wondering what he was going to do.

But once in the street, Van Damme merely touched the brim of his hat and went striding off to the right.

Taxis were rare in Liège. Maigret, unfamiliar with the trams, returned on foot to the Hôtel du Chemin de Fer, had lunch and made inquiries about the local newspapers.

At two o'clock, he went into the *Meuse* newspaper office just as Van Damme was leaving it. The two men passed within a yard of each other without a word of greeting, and the Inspector growled to himself:

'He keeps arriving ahead of me. . . .'

He went up to an official, asked if he could consult the newspaper files, and had to fill in a form and wait for an administrative permit.

Certain details had struck him: Armand Lecocq d'Arneville had learnt that his brother had left Liège at more or less the time that Jef Lombard was drawing hanged men with such morbid persistence.

And *Clothing B*, which the Neuschanz and Bremen vagrant was carrying about in his yellow suitcase, was very old – at least six years, according to the German expert – maybe ten!

On top of which, wasn't Joseph Van Damme's presence at the *Meuse* office enough to tell the Inspector something?

He was shown into a room with a parquet floor which shone like a skating-rink, containing formal but luxurious furniture.

The official with his silver chain asked him:

'Which year's numbers do you wish to consult?'

Maigret had already spotted the enormous cardboard files, each containing a year's issues, ranged all round the room.

'I can find them myself,' he said.

There was a smell of polish, old papers, and official luxury. On the imitation-leather table-top were stands designed to hold the cumbersome volumes. Everything was so clean, neat, and austere that the Inspector hardly dared take his pipe out of his pocket.

A few moments later, he was thumbing through the daily editions of the newspapers for 'the year of the hanged men'.

Thousands of headlines filed past his eyes. Some reminded him of world events. Others dealt with local matters: a fire at a big store (a whole page three days running), an alderman's resignation, a rise in the cost of railway fares.

Suddenly he saw some torn scraps of paper sticking out of the binding. One paper – that of 15 February – had been ripped out.

Maigret hurried into the waiting-room and fetched the official.

'There was someone here before me, wasn't there? Was this the file he asked for?'

'Yes. He only stayed here five minutes.'

'Are you from Liège? Do you remember what happened on that date?'

'Let's see. Ten years ago . . . That was the year my sister-in-law died. I've got it! There were some big floods. In fact, we had to wait a week for the burial, because you could

71

only move round the streets near the Meuse by boat. Anyway, look at the articles. *The King and Queen visit the victims.* There are some photos. Hullo! There's a number missing! That's extraordinary! I'll have to report that to the Director. . . .'

Maigret bent down and picked up a scrap of newspaper which had fallen when Joseph Van Damme had, without a shadow of a doubt, torn out the pages relating to 15 February.

CHAPTER 7

The Trio

THERE are four daily newspapers in Liège. It took Maigret two hours to go round their offices and, as he expected, in each he found a number missing from the files: the one for 15 February.

The town was at its busiest in the rectangle of streets called the Carré, where the luxury stores, the large *brasseries*, the cinemas and dance-halls are.

It is a popular meeting-place and, at least three times, the Inspector saw Joseph Van Damme walking around, stick in hand.

When he went back to the Hôtel du Chemin de Fer, there were two messages waiting for him. The first was a telegram from Lucas, to whom he had confided various jobs just as he was leaving.

Ashes found in stove room Louis Jeunet rue Roquette examined by expert stop identified remains Belgian and French banknotes stop quantity indicates large sum

The other was a letter which had been brought to the hotel by messenger. It was typed on ordinary typing-paper. It said:

Sir,
It is my honour to inform you that I am ready to provide any information which may help the inquiry which you have undertaken.

For various reasons, I have to be careful but, if my proposal interests you, I would be grateful if we could meet this evening, about eleven o'clock, at the Café de la Bourse, behind the Théâtre Royal.

In the meantime, I remain, Sir, etc. . . .

No signature. On the other hand, it was rather unusual language, typical business jargon, for a note of this kind:

'It is my honour to inform you . . . I would be grateful . . .
If my proposal interests you . . . In the meantime, I remain . . .'

Maigret dined alone and realized that, almost without
knowing it, the general drift of his preoccupations had
changed. He was thinking less about Jean Lecocq d'Arneville, alias Louis Jeunet, who had killed himself in a hotel
bedroom in Bremen.

But he was haunted by Jef Lombard's drawings, by the
hanged men all over on the walls, swinging from the cross
of a church, from trees in a wood, from a nail in a garret,
grotesque or sinister hanged men, scarlet or white in the
face, in costumes of all periods.

At half past ten, he set off towards the Théâtre Royal, and
it was five to eleven when he pushed open the door of the
Café de la Bourse, a quiet little place, frequented by regulars
and, in particular, by card-players.

A surprise was in store for him: In a corner by the
counter, three men were seated at a table: Maurice Belloir,
Jef Lombard, and Joseph Van Damme.

There was a moment's hesitation on both sides while the
waiter helped the Inspector off with his overcoat. Belloir,
automatically half rose to greet him. Van Damme did not
stir. Lombard, who looked incredibly nervous, was fidgeting on his chair, waiting for his companions to decide on
some attitude.

Would Maigret walk over to them, shake hands, and sit
down at their table? He knew them. He had lunched with
the Bremen business-man. Belloir had given him a glass of
brandy at his house in Rheims. And Jef had had him in his
house that same morning. . . .

'Good evening, gentlemen. . . .'

He shook hands with his usual vigour, which at times
seemed almost menacing.

'Fancy meeting you again!'

There was an empty place on the seat alongside Van
Damme, so he sat down and said to the waiter:

'A light beer!'

Then there was silence, a heavy, unnatural silence. Van Damme stared out straight in front of him, his jaws clenched. Jef Lombard was still fidgeting, as if his clothes were too tight at the armholes. Belloir, stiff and aloof, was examining his nails and running a bit of match under the nail of his first finger to remove some dirt.

'Is Madame Lombard all right?'

Jef Lombard looked round, as if for support, then stared at the stove and stammered:

'Very well. Thank you. . . .'

There was a clock above the counter and Maigret counted a good five minutes before a word was spoken. Van Damme had let his cigar go out and was the only one to let his face wear a look of undisguised hatred.

Jef was the most interesting to watch. The events of the day had obviously conspired to set his nerves on edge. There wasn't a muscle in his face, however small, that wasn't twitching.

The four men's table was a complete oasis of silence in the café, where all the others were talking at the tops of their voices.

'*Belote* again!' someone called triumphantly from the right.

'*Tierce* high!' said another from the left rather doubtfully. 'Is it good?'

'Three beers! Three!' yelled the waiter.

Everything was alive and humming except the table where the four men were sitting, which seemed gradually to be surrounded by an invisible wall.

It was Jef who broke the spell. He bit his lower lip and got up, stammering:

'What the hell!'

He gave his companions a short, sharp, unhappy glance, took down his coat and hat, went to the door, and wrenched it open.

'I bet he's going to burst into tears,' mused Maigret.

He had sensed that sob of rage and desperation which had welled up in the photo-engraver's throat and made his Adam's apple quiver.

He turned towards Van Damme, who was examining the marble table-top, swallowed half his glass of beer, and wiped his lips with the back of his hand.

It was the same atmosphere, only ten times stronger, as in the house in Rheims, where Maigret had already forced himself on the same people. The Inspector's massive bulk helped to lend an air of menace to his imposed presence.

He was tall and broad, especially broad, thick and solid, and his rather ordinary clothes emphasized his rather plebeian build. He had a heavy face, and his eyes could remain bovine and motionless.

He was, in fact, like one of those figures in a child's nightmares with enormously large expressionless eyes who bear down on the sleeper as if to crush him.

It was something implacable, inhuman, like an elephant moving relentlessly towards its goal.

He was drinking, smoking his pipe, and gazing contentedly at the hand of the clock as it jerked forward, each minute, with a metallic click. An insipid clock.

He did not seem to be watching anyone in particular and yet he was on the look-out for the slightest sign of life left and right of him.

It was one of the most extraordinary hours in his career. In fact it lasted nearly an hour. Fifty-two minutes to be precise. A war of nerves.

Jef Lombard had been put out of action at the start. But the other two were hanging on.

There he was, between them, like a judge, but a judge who made no accusations and whose thoughts could not be read. What did he know? Why had he come? What was he doing? Was he waiting for the word or the gesture which would confirm his suspicions? Had he already found out the truth or was his self-assurance mere bluff?

What could any of them say? Talk again about a coincidence, a chance meeting?

Silence reigned. They were waiting, not even knowing what they were waiting for. They were waiting for something, yet nothing happened.

The hand of the clock shuddered forward every minute. There was a slight creak from the works. At first, they did not hear it. Now, it was deafening. There were three distinct parts to the movement: a first click, then the hand starting to move; then another click as if it were settling itself in its new place. And the face of the clock changed; the obtuse angle gradually became an acute angle. The two hands were about to coincide.

The waiter kept looking at their gloomy table in astonishment. Monsieur Belloir swallowed now and again. Maigret did not have to look at him to know what he was doing. He could hear him existing, breathing, going tense, and sometimes shifting his feet carefully, as if in church.

The customers were thinning out. The red cloths and cards disappeared from the tables and their pale marble-tops appeared. The waiter went out to pull down the shutters, while the manageress arranged the counters in small piles, according to their value.

'Are you staying on?' Belloir asked, his voice almost unrecognizable.

'How about you?'

'I . . . I don't know. . . .'

Then Van Damme rapped the table with a coin and asked the waiter:

'How much?'

'The round? Nine francs seventy-five. . . .'

All three were standing up, avoiding each other's eyes. The waiter helped them on with their coats.

'Good night, gentlemen.'

It was foggy outside and they could hardly see the lights of the street-lamps. All the shutters were closed. Somewhere in the distance, footsteps echoed along the pavement.

No one could decide which way to go. None of the three men wanted to take the responsibility for leading the way. Behind them, the door of the café was being locked and safety bars secured.

An alleyway, with a crooked row of old houses, led off to the left.

'Well, gentlemen,' said Maigret finally, 'all that remains is to wish you a good night. . . .'

Belloir's hand, which he shook first, was cold and nervous. Van Damme's, which he held out unwillingly, was moist and flabby.

The Inspector turned up his coat collar, gave a little cough, and began to walk alone, down the deserted street. All his senses were directed towards one object: he was listening for the merest sound, the least disturbance in the air which would warn him of danger.

His right hand was in his pocket, gripping the butt of his revolver. It seemed as if, in the network of alleyways which spread away to his left, isolated in Liège like a leper-colony, people were walking along hurriedly, trying not to make a noise.

He caught a low murmur of conversation, either very far away or very close to, he couldn't tell, because the fog was playing tricks with his senses.

Then, suddenly, he flung himself to one side, and flattened himself against a door. There was a muffled explosion and someone made off at full speed in the darkness.

Maigret walked forward a few steps, peered into the alleyway from which the shot had come, saw nothing but some dark patches which evidently led into blind alleys and, right at the end, two hundred yards away, a frosted-glass globe, a sign over a fish-and-chip shop.

A few moments later, he passed the shop. A girl walked out of it with a bagful of golden-brown chips. She made him a half-hearted proposition, and went off towards a better-lit street.

*

Maigret was writing away peacefully, pressing his pen on the paper with his huge index finger and, from time to time, ramming down the hot ash in his pipe.

He was in his room in the Hôtel du Chemin de Fer. The brightly-lit station-clock, which he could see through the window, said two in the morning.

Dear Lucas,

As one never knows how things will turn out, here are a few notes, which would enable you, should the need arise, to carry on with the inquiry I have begun.

(1) Last week, in Brussels, a shabbily-dressed man, looking like a tramp, made up a parcel of about thirty thousand-franc notes, and sent them to his own address in the rue de la Roquette, Paris. Inquiries will show that he often sent himself sums of this order, *but that he did not make use of them himself*. The proof is that the ashes of a large number of notes, deliberately burned, were found in his room.

He went by the name of Louis Jeunet and worked fairly regularly in a workshop in the same street.

He was married (see Madame Jeunet, herbalist, rue Picpus) and had one child. But he left his wife and child in unhappy circumstances, after some severe bouts of drunkenness.

In Brussels, after sending off the money, he bought a suitcase in which to put some things he was keeping in a hotel bedroom. I exchanged this suitcase for another, while he was on his way to Bremen.

Jeunet, *who did not seem to have considered suicide till then, and had bought something to eat for supper*, noticed that his things had been filched from him, and killed himself.

The object in question was an old suit which did not belong to him and which, some years earlier, had been torn during a struggle and soaked with blood. *The suit was made in Liège*.

In Bremen, a man came to see the corpse. His name was Joseph Van Damme, an import–export agent, *born in Liège*.

Back in Paris, I learnt that Louis Jeunet was, in fact, Jean Lecocq d'Arneville, *born in Liège*, who has not been heard of for a long time. He studied and even went to University. In Liège, from which he disappeared about ten years ago, there was nothing against him.

(2) In Rheims, Jean Lecocq d'Arneville was seen, one night before he left for Brussels, entering the house of Maurice Belloir, vice-chairman of a bank, *born in Liège*; the latter denied this meeting.

But the thirty thousand francs sent from Brussels have been traced to this same Belloir.

At Belloir's house I met: Van Damme, who had flown in from Bremen, Jef Lombard, a photo-engraver from Liège, and Gaston Janin, also *born in that town*.

As I was returning to Paris with Van Damme, he tried to push me into the Marne.

I found him again in Liège, at Jef Lombard's. The latter, ten years ago, spent his time painting, and the walls of his house are covered with drawings from that period representing hanged men.

In the newspaper offices I visited, the 15 February editions of the year of the hanged men had been torn out by Van Damme.

That evening, an unsigned letter promised me a complete explanation, and fixed a rendezvous in a café in the town. There I found not one man, but three: Belloir (who had come from Rheims), Van Damme, and Jef Lombard.

They greeted me with embarrassment. I am convinced that one of the three had decided to talk. The others seemed to be there merely to prevent him.

Jef Lombard, who was on edge, suddenly cleared off. I remained with the two others. I left them outside, after midnight, in the fog, and, a few seconds later, a shot was fired at me.

I concluded that one of the three had wanted to talk and also that one of the three had tried to get me out of the way.

It is obvious that, since this amounts to a confession of guilt, *the person concerned has only one course – to try again and not miss me.*

But which is it? Belloir, Van Damme, or Lombard?

I shall find out when he tries again. Since there may be an accident, I am taking the precaution of sending you these notes which will enable you to pick up the threads of the inquiry from the beginning.

As to the psychological aspect of the case, pay special attention to Madame Jeunet and Armand Lecocq, the dead man's brother.

I am now going to bed. My regards to everyone back there.

MAIGRET

*

The fog had cleared, leaving beads of white hoar-frost on the trees and every blade of grass in the Square d'Avroy, which Maigret was crossing.

A watery sun was shining in the pale blue sky, and the frost was gradually melting into little drops of clear water which were falling on to the gravel.

It was eight in the morning when the Inspector strode through the still-deserted Carré where the cinema billboards were leaning against closed shutters. Maigret stopped at a letter-box, dropped in his letter to Sergeant Lucas, and looked around him with a flicker of anxiety.

In this same town, in these same streets, bathed in pale sunshine, a man, at that same moment, was thinking about him, a man whose only hope of safety was to kill him. He had an advantage over the Inspector in that he knew the ground, as he had proved that night when he plunged into the tangle of alleyways.

He knew Maigret, too. Perhaps he was even watching him at that very moment, whereas the Inspector was unaware of his identity.

Was it Jef Lombard? Was the danger in that old house in the rue Hors-Château, where the woman and her baby were sleeping on the first floor, cared for by her good mother, while the unruffled workmen moved from one tray of acid to another, hustled by cyclist messengers from the newspapers?

Was it perhaps Joseph Van Damme, savage and morose, bold and scheming, who was spying on the Inspector from a place *to which he knew he would eventually come?*

Ever since Bremen, the latter had anticipated everything! Three lines in the German newspapers, and he had hurried along to the mortuary. He had lunched with Maigret and yet had arrived in Rheims before him.

He was the first in the rue Hors-Château. He had arrived at the newspaper offices before him.

Finally, he was at the Café de la Bourse.

It was true that there was nothing to prove that he

wasn't the one who wanted to talk. But nothing proved the contrary!

Perhaps it was Belloir, cold, formal, with all the arrogance of the upper-middle-class provincial. Perhaps he was the one whose only hope was to dispose of Maigret?

Or was it Gaston Janin, the little sculptor with the goatee? He had not been at the Café de la Bourse, but he could have been on the watch in the street.

How did it all link up with a hanged man swinging from the cross on a church? With those dozens of hanged men? With the forests of trees which bore no fruit but hanged men? With an old blood-stained suit, ripped at the lapels by frenzied nails?

The typists were going off to work. A municipal motor-sweeper was crawling along, with its two mechanical water jets, and its roller-shaped broom which swept the rubbish into the gutter.

At the street-corners, the town police, in their white enamel helmets, could be seen directing the traffic with their shiny white arms.

'Where's the main police-station?' Maigret inquired.

He was shown the way. He arrived while the charwomen were still busy cleaning, but a breezy clerk welcomed his fellow-policeman and, when the latter asked to see some police reports from ten years back, explaining that it was the month of February that interested him, he exclaimed:

'You're the second in twenty-four hours. You want to know if a certain Joséphine Bollant committed larceny about then, don't you?'

'Was there someone here?'

'Yesterday, about five in the afternoon. A fellow from Liège, who's done all right for himself abroad, even though he's still quite young. His father was a doctor. While he's got a nice business in Germany. . . .'

'Joseph Van Damme?'

'That's him! But he was wasting his time looking through the file, he couldn't find what he wanted. . . .'

'Will you show it me?'

It was a green file, where the daily reports were kept bound, in numerical order. There had been five reports on 15 February: two for drunkenness and rowdiness at night, one for shop-lifting, one for assault and battery, and the last for breaking and entering and stealing rabbits.

Maigret did not even read them. He looked at the numbers at the tops of the forms.

'Did Monsieur Van Damme examine the book himself?' he inquired.

'Yes. He sat in the office next door.'

'Thank you.'

The five reports were numbered: 237, 238, 239, 241, and 242.

In other words, one was missing and had been torn out, just as the newspapers had been torn from their files: it was No. 240.

A few minutes later, Maigret was out in the square behind the Hôtel de Ville, where cars were arriving for a wedding. In spite of himself, he had his ear cocked for the least sound; he was a shade nervous and was not enjoying it.

CHAPTER 8

Little Émile Klein

HE had timed it just right! It was nine o'clock. The staff were arriving at the Town Hall and crossing the main courtyard, pausing a moment to say good morning to each other on the handsome stone steps at the top of which a concierge with a braided cap and well-trimmed beard was smoking a pipe.

It was a meerschaum. Maigret noted the detail, for no special reason, possibly because the morning sun was reflected in it and because it was already seasoned. For a moment the Inspector envied the man, smoking away with greedy little puffs; he seemed like a symbol of peace and well-being.

The air was alive that morning, and became still more so as the sun rose in the sky. There was a glorious cacophony, shouts in Walloon dialect, the harsh clanging of the red and yellow trams, and the quadruple jets of an enormous fountain dominated by a Liège-style flight of steps, which was doing its best to drown the clamour of the nearby market.

Maigret saw Joseph Van Damme go up one side of the double staircase and disappear into the entrance-hall.

The Inspector hurried after him. Inside, the staircase went on up on two sides, meeting again on each floor. The two men came face to face on one of the landings, out of breath from running, and trying to appear natural to an official wearing a silver chain.

It was all very quick and poignant. A matter of precision, of a split second.

As he went up the staircase, Maigret had assumed that Van Damme had come there, as to the newspaper offices and the police station, simply to make something disappear.

One of the reports for 15 February had already been torn out.

But surely, as is the practice in most towns, the police would have sent the mayor a copy of the daily reports every morning?

'I should like to see the Town Clerk,' announced Maigret with van Damme only six feet away. 'It's urgent. . . .'

Their eyes met. They wondered whether to shake hands, decided not to and, when the official asked him what he wanted, the Bremen business-man simply murmured:

'It's nothing. I'll come back. . . .'

He went off. His footsteps grew fainter in the entrance-hall. Shortly afterwards, Maigret was shown into a luxurious office where the Town Clerk, buttoned up in his morning coat and high collar, set about finding the ten-year-old daily reports.

The air was warm and the carpets thick. A ray of sunshine lit up a bishop's crozier in a historical painting which occupied an entire panel on one of the walls.

After half an hour's search and an exchange of courtesies, Maigret discovered the reference to the stolen rabbits, and the reports for drunkenness and shoplifting. Then, between two miscellaneous items, came the following lines:

Police Constable Lacasse of No. 6 Division, was proceeding at six o'clock this morning to the Pont des Arches to take up point-duty and was passing the main door of the Church of Saint-Pholien, when he observed a body hanging from the door-knocker.

A doctor was urgently summoned but could only confirm the person's death, a man by the name of Émile Klein, a house-painter, twenty years old, born in Angleur and living in the rue du Pot-au-Noir.

Klein had apparently hanged himself, about the middle of the night, with a sash-cord. In his pockets were found only a few valueless objects and some small change.

Inquiries revealed that he had not been regularly employed for three months, and his action seems to have been the result of poverty.

His mother, Madame Klein, a widow, who lives on a modest pension in Angleur, has been notified.

*

Hours of feverish activity followed. Maigret plunged head-long down this new track. Yet, without altogether realizing it, he was less concerned with information about Klein than with meeting Van Damme.

Only if and when he came face to face with the business-man again, would he be anywhere near the truth. It had all begun in Bremen. And since then, every time the Inspector moved on a square, he had run into Van Damme.

The latter had seen him at the Town Hall, knew that he had read the report, and that he was on Klein's tracks.

Angleur produced nothing. The Inspector took a taxi into an industrial area of small, identical working-class houses, all the same sooty grey colour, in mean streets beneath the factory chimneys.

A woman was washing the doorstep of one of the houses, the one where Madame Klein had lived.

'She's been dead at least five years. . . .'

The shadow of Van Damme did not fall round there.

'Didn't her son live with her?'

'No. He came to a sticky end. He did away with himself on a church door. . . .'

That was all. Maigret merely learnt that Klein's father was a foreman in a coal mine and that, after his death, his wife lived on a small pension, sub-let the house, and only occupied an attic-room in it.

'To No. 6 Police Division,' he told the driver.

Constable Lagasse was still alive. But he barely remem-bered anything.

'It had been raining all night. He was soaked through and his red hair was plastered all over his face.'

'Was he tall? Or small?'

'On the small side.'

Then the Inspector went to the gendarmerie and spent

nearly an hour in their offices which smelt of leather and sweating horses.

'If he was twenty at the time, he must have gone before a military board. You did say Klein with a K?'

They found sheet No. 13 in the 'rejected' file. Maigret copied down the figures: *height* five foot two, *chest* thirty-two, and a note about '*weak lungs*'.

But there was still no clue leading to Van Damme. He was clearly to be found somewhere else. The only result of the morning's calls was to establish that *Suit B* had never belonged to the hanged man of Saint-Pholien, who was a little shrimp.

Klein had committed suicide. There had been no struggle and not a drop of blood had been spilt.

So where was the link with the Bremen tramp's suitcase and the death of Lecocq d'Arneville, alias Louis Jeunet?

*

'Drop me here. And tell me how to find the rue du Pot-au-Noir.'

'Behind the church. The one leading into the Quai Sainte-Barbe.'

When he arrived in front of Saint-Pholien, Maigret paid off the taxi. He was now looking at the new church which stood in the middle of a vast stretch of waste land.

To right and left of it were broad streets flanked by blocks of flats, about the same age as the church. But behind the latter, there was still an old district which had been partially demolished to make room for the church.

In a stationer's window Maigret found some picture-postcards of the old church, which was lower, squatter, and black all over. One wing was shored up with timbers. On three sides, low, sordid-looking houses backed on to its walls, giving the whole place a medieval appearance.

Nothing remained now of this courtyard of Miracles except a jumble of houses, separated by narrow streets and blind alleys, and pervaded by a nauseating stench of poverty.

The rue du Pot-au-Noir was barely two yards wide and down the middle of it flowed a stream of soapy water. Children were playing on the doorsteps. Inside, it was swarming with humanity.

It was dark in spite of the sun, which was bright but could not penetrate down the alleyway. A cooper had lit a brazier out in the street and was hooping barrels.

The numbers of the houses had completely faded. The Inspector had to inquire. When he asked for No. 7, he was shown a courtyard, from which came a noise of saws and planes.

On the far side was a workshop, with several carpenter's benches, at which three men were working. All the doors were open and glue was being melted on a stove.

One of the men looked up, put down his cigarette-end and waited for the visitor to speak.

'Did someone called Klein live here?'

The man looked round knowingly at his companions, pointed to a door and a dark staircase, and muttered:

'Up that way! There's someone already there.'

'A new tenant?'

He replied with an odd smile, which the Inspector only understood later on.

'Go and have a look. It's on the first floor. You can't miss it: it's the only door. . . .'

One of the workmen laughed softly as he worked his plane. Maigret started up the staircase in total darkness. A few steps up, the banisters were missing.

He struck a match and saw above him a door with no lock or handle; it seemed to be secured by a string tied to a rusty nail.

His hand in his revolver pocket, he pushed open the door with his knee, and was dazzled by the light which streamed through a stained-glass window with a third of its panes broken.

What Maigret saw was so unexpected that he looked around him for a moment before he could make out any details. Finally, in a corner, he saw a shape, a man leaning against the wall, fixing him with a savage glare: it was Joseph Van Damme.

'We were bound to end up here, weren't we?' declared the Inspector.

His voice echoed strangely in the stark, empty atmosphere.

Van Damme did not reply, but remained quite still, staring at him viciously.

*

It would have been impossible to understand the geography of the place unless you knew what type of building it had once been: part of a convent, a barracks, or a private house.

Nothing in it was square. Half the floor was boarded and the other half was made up of crooked flagstones, as in some old chapel.

The walls were white-washed, except for a rectangle of brown-coloured brick which presumably blocked up an old window. Through the stained-glass window could be seen a gable, a piece of guttering, and come crooked roofs in the background, in the direction of the Meuse.

But that was the least unexpected. The oddest thing was the complete illogicality of its contents, evocative of the mad-house or some huge practical joke.

Pell-mell on the floor were new, unfinished chairs, a door lying full length, with a mended panel, some pots of glue, broken saws, and boxes, from which straggled straw and shavings.

By contrast, in one corner, there was a kind of divan, or rather a spring mattress, partly covered with a piece of cretonne. Just above it dangled an odd-shaped lantern, with coloured glass, the sort sometimes to be seen in junk-shops.

Sections of an incomplete skeleton, the kind used by students, had been flung down on the divan. The ribs and the pelvis were still attached by hooks and were leaning forward like a rag doll.

Then there were the walls. The white walls had been covered with drawings, and painted frescoes.

This was the most incongruous aspect of the muddle: there were grimacing figures and inscriptions like *Long live Satan, grandfather of the world!*

On the floor was a Bible with a damaged cover. Elsewhere were crumpled sketches and yellowing papers, covered with a thick layer of dust.

There was another inscription over the door: *Welcome to the Damned!*

In the middle of all this rubbish, were the unfinished chairs, which smelt of the carpenter's shop, the glue-pots and rough deal planks, and an overturned stove, red with rust.

Finally, there was Joseph Van Damme, with his well-cut overcoat, carefully-shaved face, and impeccable shoes, Van Damme, who was still the man of the large Bremen brasseries, modern office-blocks, expensive dinners and glasses of old Armagnac. . . .

. . . Van Damme who drove his car and greeted important people, pointing out that the one in the fur coat was worth millions and that another had thirty cargo-boats on the high seas, and who, a little later, to the accompaniment of light music and the clinking of glasses and saucers, went and shook hands with all these magnates, feeling that he would soon be their equal. . . .

Van Damme suddenly looked like a hunted beast, motionless, his back still against the wall, the plaster whitening his shoulders, one hand in his overcoat pocket, glowering at Maigret.

'How much?'

Had he in fact spoken? Could the Inspector, in that fantastic atmosphere, have been the victim of a delusion?

He gave a start and upset a seatless chair, making a clatter.

Van Damme was scarlet in the face. Yet he had lost his healthy glow. There was panic, or desperation, as well as fury and the will to live, to triumph no matter what the cost, in his tensed-up features, in his expression, as he screwed up his last powers of resistance.

'What do you mean?'

Maigret went over to a pile of crumpled sketches which had been swept into a corner under the stained-glass window. Before getting an answer, he had time to spread out some nude sketches of a girl with coarse features and untidy hair, a vigorous well-formed body, swollen breasts, and broad hips.

'There's still time,' Van Damme went on. 'Fifty thousand? A hundred? . . .'

The Inspector glanced at him curiously. With barely concealed anxiety, the latter snapped:

'Two hundred thousand!'

There was fear in the air within the crooked walls of the wretched hovel. It was acrid, unhealthy, morbid.

Perhaps it was something more than fear: a repressed desire, a mad urge to kill. . . .

However, Maigret went on thumbing through the old papers, and found the same voluptuous girl, in different poses. As she posed, she seemed to have been gazing sullenly in front of her.

Once, the artist had tried draping her in the piece of cretonne which lay over the divan. On another occasion, he had drawn her in black stockings.

Behind her was a skull, which now lay at the foot of the spring mattress. Maigret remembered seeing this macabre head in one of Jef Lombard's portraits.

Links were forming, though still confusedly, between people and events, through time and space. With a somewhat nervous gesture, the Inspector spread out a new charcoal sketch which showed a young man with long hair, his shirt open across his chest, and on his chin the first signs of a beard.

He, too, was in a romantic pose. His head was three-quarters on, and seemed to be gazing into the future, as an eagle stares at the sun.

It was Jean Lecocq d'Arneville, who had committed suicide in that sordid Bremen hotel, the tramp who had not eaten his sausage-rolls.

'Two hundred thousand francs!'

Though it still betrayed the business-man, concerned with the slightest details and fluctuations of currency, the voice added:

'French francs! . . . Look, Inspector . . .'

Maigret sensed that pleading would soon give way to threats, and that the fear which throbbed in his voice would not take long to change into a growl of rage.

'There's still time. No official action has been taken. We're in Belgium. . . .'

There was still a stump of candle in the lamp and the Inspector found an old paraffin-stove under the piles of papers on the floor.

'You are not on official business. And even . . . Give me a month. . . .'

'In other words, it happened in December. . . .'

Van Damme seemed to huddle closer to the wall. He stammered:

'What do you mean?'

'It is now November. In February, it will be ten years since Klein hanged himself. But you're only asking me for a month. . . .'

'I don't understand. . . .'

'Yes, you do!'

It was maddening to see Maigret still turning over the old papers with his left hand – the papers crackling as they brushed against each other – while his right hand remained thrust deep into his overcoat pocket.

'You understand quite well, Van Damme. If it were a question of Klein's death and if, for instance, he had been murdered, the time-limit would only come into force in

February, in other words, ten years afterwards. Yet you're only asking for a month. So it must have happened in December. . . .'

'You won't find anything. . . .'

His voice quavered, like a faulty gramophone.

'Then why are you frightened?'

He lifted up the springs of the bed. There was nothing underneath except dust and a barely identifiable crust of mouldy bread.

'Two hundred thousand francs. We could arrange it so that, later on . . .'

'Do you want your face slapped?'

It was so violent and unexpected, that for a moment Van Damme lost control, moved as if to protect himself, and, as he did so, unintentionally pulled out the automatic which he was gripping in his overcoat pocket.

He realized what he had done; for a second madness took hold of him but he couldn't bring himself to shoot.

'Drop that!'

His fingers opened. The automatic dropped to the floor near a pile of shavings.

Maigret turned his back on the enemy and continued to ferret about in the fantastic mass of heterogeneous objects. He picked up a sock which was also yellow and blotched with mildew.

'Tell me, Van Damme . . .'

He turned round, sensing something unusual in the air. He saw the man run his hand over his cheek and his fingers leave a damp streak.

'Are you crying?'

'Me?'

The *me* was aggressive, sardonic, desperate.

'Which branch of the army were you in?'

The other did not understand. He was ready to clutch at any straw of hope.

'I was in the E.S.L.R. The School for Reserve Second Lieutenants, at Beverloo. . . .'

'Infantry?'

'Cavalry.'

'In other words, you were then between five foot six and five foot eight. And you weighed under ten stone. So you must have filled out since. . . .'

Maigret pushed back a chair he had knocked into, picked up another scrap of paper, apparently part of a letter, with only one line on it:

My dear old friend . . .

But he kept watching Van Damme, who was trying to understand. Then, suddenly guessing, in hopeless confusion and his face contorted, he exclaimed:

'It wasn't me! I swear I've never worn that suit!'

Maigret gave his companion's revolver a kick and sent it skidding across to the other side of the room.

Why did he count up the children again just then? A small boy at Belloir's. Three kids in the rue Hors-Château, the last of whom had hardly opened its eyes. And the so-called Louis Jeunet's son.

On the floor lay an unsigned pastel sketch of the beautiful naked girl, arching her back.

There were hesitant footsteps on the stairs. A hand fumbled at the door, groping for the string which acted as a latch.

CHAPTER 9

The Companions of the Apocalypse

IN the scene which followed, everything counted: words, silences, looks, even the involuntary twitch of a muscle. Everything was fraught with meaning, and behind the actors loomed the stark ghost of fear.

The door opened. Maurice Belloir appeared. He glanced first at Van Damme, huddled against the wall in one corner, and then at the automatic lying on the floor.

It was enough. He understood. Especially when he saw Maigret, his pipe between his teeth, still calmly thumbing through the old sketches.

'Lombard's coming!' Belloir blurted out, though it was not clear whether he was addressing the Inspector or his companion. 'I took a cab . . .'

These words alone were enough to show Maigret that the vice-chairman of the bank had thrown up the sponge. It was barely perceptible. His face was less strained, but there were tired and guilty inflexions in his voice.

All three looked at each other. Joseph Van Damme began:

'What's he . . .'

'He's like a madman. I tried to calm him down. But he got away. He went off, talking to himself and waving his arms. . . .'

'With a gun?' Maigret inquired.

'With a gun. . . .'

Maurice Belloir was listening with the unhappy look of a man who is shattered yet is trying in vain to control himself.

'Were both of you in the rue Hors-Château? Were you waiting for the result of my conversation with . . .'

He pointed to Van Damme. Belloir nodded assent.

95

'And did all three of you agree to offer me . . .'

He did not need to finish his sentence. They knew what he was referring to. They even understood what he meant when he was not speaking. It was as if they could hear what he was thinking.

Suddenly, there were hurried steps on the stairs. Some-one stumbled, apparently fell on his face, and cursed angrily. A moment later, the door was kicked open and in the doorway stood Jef Lombard. He remained there for a moment, motionless, gazing at the three men with a terrify-ing stare.

He was shaking. He was in the grip of a fever, or perhaps some kind of madness.

Everything must have been dancing before his eyes, the figure of Belloir as he drew away from him, Van Damme's flushed face, and finally Maigret, with his broad shoulders, holding his breath and not stirring a finger.

To cap it all, there was all that fantastic junk, scattered drawings, and the naked girl, with only her chin and breasts showing, the lamp and the battered divan.

The scene could only have lasted a fraction of a second. At the end of Jef's long arm was a revolver.

Maigret watched him calmly. Even so, he heaved a sigh of relief when Jef Lombard threw the gun to the ground, clasped his head in his hands, broke into loud sobs, and groaned:

'I can't! I can't! Do you understand? I can't, damn it!'

He leant both arms against the wall, his shoulders were heaving, and he was sniffing audibly.

The Inspector went and shut the door because they could hear the noise of sawing and planing, as well as of kids squealing in the distance.

*

Jef Lombard wiped his face with his handkerchief, flicked back his hair, and looked round him with the vacant stare that people have after a nervous breakdown.

He had not yet entirely calmed down. His fingers were twitching. His nostrils were quivering. When he tried to speak, he had to bite his lip because another sob was welling up.

'To come to this!' he said in a voice made flat and cutting by sarcasm.

He tried to laugh, a desperate laugh.

'Nine years! Almost ten! I was left on my own, without a sou, and without a job. . . .'

He was talking to himself, no doubt unaware that he was staring hard at the picture of the nude – flesh in the raw.

'Ten years of daily grind, failure and difficulties of every sort! Yet I married. I wanted kids. I worked like a black to give them a decent life. A house, the workshop, everything. You saw it all. But what you didn't see were my efforts to build it all up. The discouragements. The bills at the beginning, which used to keep me awake at night. . . .'

He swallowed and ran his hand across his forehead. His Adam's apple rose and fell.

'So, anyway, I've just got a little daughter. I'm not sure if I've even looked at her! My wife, who's still in bed, doesn't understand, and stares at me, terrified, because she no longer recognizes me. The workmen keep asking me things and I don't know what to tell them. . . .

'Washed up! In a few days, suddenly! Undermined, destroyed, broken, smashed to bits! Everything! Ten years' work!

'And all because of . . .'

He clenched his fists, looked at the gun on the floor, and then at Maigret. He was at his wit's end.

'Let's get it over with!' he sighed, with a gesture of weariness. 'Who's going to do the talking? It's all so stupid!'

His words seemed to be addressed to the skull, to the piles of old sketches, and to the extravagant drawings on the walls.

'So stupid!' he repeated.

He looked as if he were going to cry again. But no. He was played out. The crisis was over. He went and sat on the edge of the divan, rested his elbows on his bony knees, cupped his chin in his hands, and stayed there, waiting.

He only moved to scratch a spot of mud off one of his trouser turn-ups with his nail.

*

'Am I disturbing you?'

It was a cheerful voice. The carpenter entered, covered in sawdust, glanced at the drawings decorating the walls, and then burst out laughing.

'So you came back to see all that?'

No one moved. Belloir was the only one who tried to appear natural.

'You remember you still owe me the twenty francs from last month? Oh, I haven't come to ask for them. I can't help laughing because, when you went away and left all this old rubbish, I remember you saying:

'"Maybe some day, a single one of these sketches will be worth more than this whole hovel put together. . . ."'

'I didn't believe it. Mind you, I held off painting the walls. One day, I brought along a frame-maker who sells pictures, and he took away two or three of the drawings. He gave me a hundred sous. Are you still painting?'

Eventually, he realized that there was something unusual going on. Joseph Van Damme was gazing stubbornly at the floor. Belloir was snapping his fingers impatiently.

'Wasn't it you who started a business in the Rue Hors-Château?' the carpenter went on to ask Jef. 'I've a nephew who worked for you. A tall, fair fellow. . . .'

'Possibly . . .' Jef sighed, looking away.

'I don't recognize you. Were you in the gang?'

The owner was addressing Maigret.

'No.'

'A weird crew! My wife didn't want me to let the place, then she advised me to sling them out, especially as they often didn't pay. But it amused me. First, it was which one could wear the biggest hat, then who could smoke the longest clay pipe! And they used to spend whole nights singing and drinking. There were some pretty girls here sometimes. By the way, Monsieur Lombard, do you know what became of the one on the ground there?'

'She married an inspector in the "Grand Bazar", and she now lives a hundred yards down the road. She's got a son who's at school with mine. . . .'

Lombard got up, walked over to the stained-glass window, and came back again, in such a state that the man decided to beat a retreat.

'Perhaps I'm disturbing you? I'll leave you to it. You know, if there's anything here that interests you . . . Naturally, I never meant to keep them because of the twenty francs. All I took was a landscape for my dining-room. . . .'

Out on the landing, he looked as if he were going to embark on a fresh speech. But he was called from below.

'Someone to see you, *patron*.'

'See you later, gentlemen. Very glad to have . . .'

His voice faded as the door closed again. Maigret had lit a pipe while he was talking. The carpenter's chatter had, after all, lowered the tension somewhat. So, when the Inspector began to speak and pointed to an inscription on the wall round one of the more extravagant drawings, Maurice Belloir replied almost naturally.

The inscription was: *The Companions of the Apocalypse*.

'Was that the name of your group?'

'Yes. I'll explain. It is too late, isn't it? That's just too bad for our wives and children. . . .'

But Jef Lombard cut in:

'I want to do the talking. Let me. . . .'

He started to pace up and down the room, glancing from time to time at some object or other, as though to illustrate his story.

'A little over ten years ago, I was studying painting at the Academy. I used to wear a broad-brimmed hat and a flowing cravat. There were two others with me. Gaston Janin, who was doing sculpture, and little Émile Klein. We used to adore parading up and down the Carré. . . . We were artists, you see. Each of us thought he'd be at least a Rembrandt. . . .

'It all began idiotically. We used to read a lot, especially writers of the Romantic period. We used to get carried away. We'd swear by one writer for a week. Then we'd drop him and take up another. . . .

'Little Émile Klein, whose mother lived in Angleur, rented this studio and we used to meet here. The medieval atmosphere, especially on winter evenings, made a great impression on us. We used to sing old songs and recite Villon. . . .

'I can't remember who discovered the *Apocalypse* and insisted on reading us whole chapters from it.

'One evening, we got to know a few students: Belloir, Armand Lecocq d'Arneville, Van Damme, and a fellow named Mortier, a Jew, whose father owned a sausage-skin and tripe shop not far from here.

'We were drinking. We brought them back here to the studio. The oldest of them wasn't even twenty-two.

'It was you, Van Damme, wasn't it?'

It was doing him good to talk. His steps became less jerky, his voice less hoarse, but after his fit of weeping, his face was still blotched with red and his lips swollen.

'I think it was my idea. To found a society, a group! I'd read stories about the secret societies which existed in German universities during the last century. A club which would link Art and Science!'

He could not help sneering when he looked at the walls.

'We were full of that kind of talk. It puffed us up with pride. On the one hand, there were the three daubers, Klein, Janin, and myself. That was Art. On the other, the students. We used to drink. We drank a lot. We drank in order to get ourselves even more worked up. We used to turn down the lights so as to produce a more mysterious atmosphere.

'We used to sleep here, too, you see. . . . Some on the divan, and the others on the floor. We used to smoke pipe after pipe. The air would grow thick.

'Then we used to sing choruses. There was nearly always someone who was sick and had to go and recover in the courtyard.

'This used to happen at two or three in the morning. We'd work ourselves up into a frenzy. The wine helped – cheap wine which turned our stomachs – as we plunged into the realms of metaphysics.

'I can still see little Émile Klein. He was the most nervous. His health was bad. His mother was poor; he lived on nothing and did without food so that he could drink.

'After we'd been drinking, we felt we were real geniuses!

'The student group was a bit more reasonable, because they weren't so poor, except for Lecocq d'Arneville. Belloir used to pinch a bottle of old Burgundy or liqueur from his parents. Van Damme used to bring some cold meat.

'We were convinced that people in the street used to look at us with a mixture of admiration and terror. We'd chosen a mysterious, high-sounding name: *The Companions of the Apocalypse*.

'I don't honestly think anyone had read the *Apocalypse* right through. It was just Klein who used to recite a few passages of it by heart when he was drunk.

'We'd arranged to split the rent, but Klein was allowed to live here.

'A few girls agreed to come and pose for nothing. Pose, and other things, of course! So we used to pretend we were Bohemians, and they were little street-girls! All that nonsense. . . .

'That's one of them on the floor. Dumb as a cow. But that didn't stop us painting her as a Madonna.

'Drink, that was the main thing. Never mind the expense, we had to whip up the atmosphere. I remember Klein trying to achieve the same result by upsetting a bottle of ether on the divan.

'And all of us working ourselves up until we were drunk and saw visions!

'God Almighty!'

Jef Lombard went and pressed his forehead against the steamy window. Then he came back with a new quaver in his voice.

'By working ourselves up into a frenzy, we ended up as packs of nerves. Especially those of us who didn't eat enough. Do you see what I mean? Little Émile Klein included. A kid who didn't eat, but kept himself going with loads of drink.

'Naturally, we re-discovered the world. We had our own ideas about all the great problems! We scoffed at the middle-class, society, and all established truths. . . .

'As soon as we'd gulped down a few drinks and the air was thick with smoke, we'd bandy the craziest ideas about! A mixture of Nietzsche, Karl Marx, Moses, Confucius, and Jesus Christ.

'For instance, let's see . . . I can't remember who it was who discovered that pain didn't exist and that it was only a figment of the imagination. I was so taken with the idea that, one night, in the middle of a breathless group, I stuck the end of a penknife into the fleshy part of my arm and tried to smile. . . .

'Then there were other things. We were an Élite, a little group of Geniuses brought together by chance. We soared above the conventional world of law and prejudice.

'A handful of gods, do you see? Gods who were sometimes starving to death, but who walked the streets proudly, dismissing the passers-by with contempt.

'We used to plan the future: Lecocq d'Arneville was to be a Tolstoy. Van Damme, who was doing a boring course at the School of Economics, was to revolutionize political economy and reverse all accepted ideas on the organization of the human race.

'Each of us had his place. There were poets, painters, and future heads of state.

'All on drink! And how! In the end, we were so used to getting carried away, that we'd hardly have got here, in the light of the lamp, with the skull from which we all drank, before each of us would manage to achieve the little frenzy he wanted, on his own. . . .

'Even the more modest of us could already see a marble plaque one day on the wall of the house: *Here met the famous Companions of the Apocalypse.* . . .

'It was a challenge to see who could bring the latest book, or come up with the most far-fetched ideas.

'It's pure chance that we didn't become anarchists. We used to discuss the question, solemnly. There had been an attempted assassination in Seville. We'd read the newspaper article out loud.

'I can't remember which of us cried out: "True genius is destructive!" . . .

'So this handful of young men used to discuss the subject for hours. We used to think up ways of manufacturing bombs. We used to wonder what it would be a good idea to blow up.

'Then Little Émile Klein, who was on his sixth or seventh glass, was sick. He rolled about on the floor, and all we could think about was what we'd do if something went wrong.

'That girl was with us. Her name was Henriette. She was crying.

'What nights they were! It was a point of honour not to leave until the lamplighter had passed and put out the lamps, and we'd go off, shivering, into the grey dawn.

'The ones who were well-off would climb in through a window, eat and sleep, and more or less repair the damage of the previous night.

'But the others, like Klein, Lecocq d'Arneville, and myself would wander the streets, nibble at a roll and gaze enviously at the shop-windows.

'I had no overcoat that year because I wanted to buy a broad-brimmed hat which cost a hundred and twenty francs.

'I used to make out that cold, like everything else, was

an illusion. So, fortified by our discussions, I told my father, a good, honest gunsmith's craftsman, who died since, that love of one's parents was the worst form of selfishness, and that a child's first duty was to deny his family. . . .

'He was a widower. He used to leave for work at six in the morning just as I was coming back. In the end, he used to leave earlier so as not to meet me, because my speeches frightened him. So he'd leave me notes on the table – *There's some cold meat in the cupboard. Father.*'

Jef's voice broke for a second or two. He looked at Belloir, who was sitting on the edge of a seatless chair, staring at the floor, and then at Van Damme, who was tearing a cigar to shreds.

'There were seven of us,' Lombard said quietly. 'Seven Supermen! Seven Geniuses! Seven kids!

'Janin's still sculpting in Paris. Or at least he makes dummies for a big factory. From time to time, he works off his frustrations by doing a bust of his current girl-friend. . . .

'Belloir's in a bank. Van Damme's in business. I'm a photo-engraver.'

There was a silence charged with fear. Jef swallowed and went on, while the rings round his eyes seemed to grow darker:

'Klein hanged himself on the church-door. Lecocq shot himself in the mouth in Bremen. . . .'

Another silence. This time, Maurice Belloir, unable to sit still, got up, seemed to hesitate, and then went and stood in front of the stained-glass window. There was a peculiar sort of noise in his chest.

'And the last of you?' said Maigret. 'Mortier, wasn't it? The tripe-merchant's son.'

Lombard turned and stared at him with such frenzy that the Inspector anticipated another fit. Van Damme knocked over a chair.

'It was in December, wasn't it?'

Maigret was talking, but not missing the slightest twitch from any of his three companions.

'It'll be ten years ago in a month's time. The time-limit will expire in a month. . . .'

First he went and picked up Joseph Van Damme's automatic, and then the revolver which Jef had thrown on the floor shortly after his arrival.

He was not mistaken. Unable to hold out, Lombard clasped his head in his hands and moaned:

'My kids! My three kids!'

Then suddenly and unashamedly turning his cheeks wet with tears to the Inspector, he once again became hysterical and shouted:

'It was because of you, you, you alone, that I didn't even look at the girl, my last child. I couldn't even tell you what she's like. . . . Do you realize?'

CHAPTER 10

Christmas Eve in the Rue du Pot-au-Noir

THERE must have been a passing shower, a low, fast-moving cloud, because all the reflections of the sun suddenly vanished. And, as if someone had turned off a switch, the air became grey and dull, and everything seemed to wear a frown.

Maigret understood how those who used to meet there felt the need to soften the light with a multi-coloured lamp, make the most of the mysterious semi-darkness, and make the atmosphere heavy with a liberal supply of tobacco and drink.

He could imagine Klein waking up, the morning after those pathetic orgies, among the empty bottles, broken glasses, stale smell, and bluey-green light which filtered through the curtainless stained-glass window.

Jef Lombard was silent from exhaustion, and it was Maurice Belloir who spoke.

There was a sudden change, as if they had moved to a different wavelength. The photo-engraver had been shaken to the depths of his entire being; he was twitching, sobbing, hissing, pacing up and down; with alternating moments of agitation and calm, which could have been plotted on a graph, like a fever.

Belloir was in control, from head to foot, voice, expression, and movements; it was so obviously the result of an intense effort of will that it was painful to see.

He couldn't have cried. Or even twitched his lips. He was rigid all over.

'May I go on, Inspector? It will soon be dark and we've no light.'

It was not his fault that he brought up a material detail. Nor was it a lack of emotion. In fact, it was really his way of expressing himself.

'I think we were all sincere in our talks and discussions, and the dreams we voiced. But there were various degrees to our sincerity.

'Jef mentioned it. On the one hand, there were the rich ones, who went home afterwards and took root again in an atmosphere of security: Van Damme, Willy Mortier, and myself. Even Janin, who had everything he wanted.

'Willy Mortier was a special case, though. Here's just one instance. He was the only one who chose his mistresses from professional night-club entertainers and small-time dancers. He used to pay them. . . .

'A practical fellow. He was like his father, who arrived in Liège penniless, unashamedly chose the sausage-skin trade, and made a packet.

'Willy got five hundred francs a month pocket-money. Compared to what we all had, it was fabulous. He never set foot in the University, got his hard-up friends to take down the lectures, and passed his exams by means of "understandings" and bribes.

'He used to come here out of sheer curiosity. We had no ideas or tastes in common.

'I mean, his father used to buy pictures from artists, even though he had no time for them. He also bribed municipal councillors and even aldermen, to obtain certain favours. And he had no time for them, either. . . .

'Anyway, Willy despised us, too. He came here to measure the difference between himself, the rich boy and the rest.

'He didn't drink. He used to look disgusted at any of us who were drunk. Throughout our interminable discussions, he only came out with a few words, which were like a cold shower, words which hurt, because they dispelled all the false poetry we had managed to create.

'He loathed us and we loathed him! What's more, he was mean. Calculatedly mean. Klein didn't eat every day. One or other of us used to help him. But Mortier said:

'"I don't want there to be any money barriers between us. I don't want to be accepted just because I'm rich. . . ."

'So he gave his share and no more when we used to search in our pockets to go and fetch some drink.

'It was Lecocq d'Arneville who used to take down his lectures for him. I once heard Willy refuse to give him an advance on his work.

'He was the alien, hostile element, which you find in all groups of men.

'We tolerated him. But Klein, among others, when he was drunk, used to attack him violently and get things off his chest. Mortier, slightly pale, would listen to him contemptuously.

'I mentioned varying degrees of sincerity. The most sincere were undoubtedly Klein and Lecocq d'Arneville. They were so close, they could have been brothers. Both had had a tough childhood, and a hard-up mother. Both wanted to succeed, and were tormented by insuperable difficulties.

'So as to study in the evenings at the Academy, Klein had to work during the day as a house painter. He admitted to us that he felt giddy when he was sent up a ladder. Lecocq used to take down lectures, and give French lessons to foreign students. He often came and ate here. The stove must still be here somewhere. . . .'

It was on the floor, by the divan, and Jef kicked at it moodily.

*

Maurice Belloir, not a hair of whose well-groomed head was out of place, went on in his dull, expressionless voice:

'Since then, I've heard people in middle-class drawing-rooms in Rheims say jokingly:

'"Given certain circumstances, would you be able to kill a man?"

'Or the mandarin problem. You know. . . . *If all you had*

*to do was press an electric button and kill a very rich mandarin
in the heart of China to become his heir, would you do it? . . .*

'Here, where the most outlandish subjects were an excuse
for discussions which went on all night, the riddle of life
and death had to come up, too. . . .

'It was shortly before Christmas. A news-item in the
paper sparked it off. It had been snowing. Our ideas had to
be different from the conventional ones, you see. So we got
carried away by the theory that man is no more than a bit
of mould on the earth's crust. What do his life or death
matter? Pity is a mere disease. Big animals eat little ones.
We eat the big animals. . . .

'Lombard told you the story of the penknife. How he
stabbed himself to prove that pain didn't exist.

'Well, that night, there were three or four empty bottles
lying about on the floor, and we were solemnly discussing
the question of killing.

'After all, we were in the realms of pure theory, where
anything is permissible. We cross-examined each other.

'"Would you dare?"

'Our eyes sparkled. Unhealthy shivers ran down our
spines.

'"Why not? If life's nothing but chance, a skin disease
on the earth's crust. . . ."

'"A stranger passing in the street?"

'Klein, who was most drunk, with dark rings round his
eyes and his skin deathly pale, replied:

'"Yes!"

'We felt we were on the brink of the abyss. We were
afraid to go any further. We were playing with danger,
jesting with death, which we had conjured up and which
now seemed to be prowling round us. . . .

'Someone – I think it was Van Damme – who had been a
choirboy, sang the *Libera nos,* which priests chant over a
coffin. We joined in the chorus. We wallowed in morbidity.

'But we didn't kill anyone, that night. At four in the
morning, I jumped over the wall and went home. At eight

o'clock, I was drinking coffee in the bosom of my family. It was simply a memory, do you understand? Like the memory of some stage-play that made you shudder.

'Klein stayed on here, in the rue du Pot-au-Noir. He nursed all these ideas too long in his big, sickly, head. They were eating at him. The next few days, he showed what he was thinking by asking sudden questions.

'"Do you really think it's difficult to kill someone?"

'We didn't want to hang back. But we weren't drunk any more. We said unconvincingly:

'"Of course not!"

'We may even have got a kick out of his childish halluci-nations. But remember, we didn't want to start off any sort of drama. We were merely exploring the ground to the limit.

'When there's a fire, the onlookers, in spite of them-selves, hope it'll go on, that it'll be a "splendid fire". When the water rises newspaper readers hope for "splendid floods" which they can talk about twenty years later.

'*Something of interest. It doesn't matter what!*

'It was Christmas Eve. Everyone brought some bottles. We drank and sang songs. Klein, half tight, kept taking one or other of us aside and saying:

'"Do you think I'm capable of killing?"

'No one was worried. At midnight, no one was sober. We were talking about fetching some more bottles.

'It was just then that Willy Mortier arrived, in a dinner-jacket, with a broad white shirt-front which seemed to absorb all the light. He was pink in the face and stank of scent. He told us that he had just come from a big smart reception.

'"Go and fetch some drink!" Klein yelled at him.

'"You're drunk, my friend. I simply came to say hullo. . . ."

'"Oh, no, it was to look at us!"

'No one could have guessed what was going to happen. Yet Klein's face was more terrifying than on any other occasion when he had been drunk. He seemed quite small and thin next to the other fellow. His hair was ruffled, sweat was pouring from his forehead, and his tie was flapping.

'"You're a drunken pig, Klein!"

'"All right, so the pig says go and fetch some drink. . . ."

'I think Willy was scared at that point. He was vaguely aware that no one was laughing. Even so, he brazened it out.

'He had black curly hair that stank of scent.

'"I must say you're not exactly cheerful here," he remarked. "It was far more amusing with the stuffy crowd I came from. . . ."

'"Go and fetch some drink. . . ."

'Klein circled round him, his eyes blazing. A few of us were in one corner, discussing some theory of Kant's. Someone else was crying and swearing he wasn't fit to be alive. . . .

'No one was in control of himself. No one saw it all. Klein suddenly darted forward, a little bundle of taut nerves and struck him. . . .

'It looked as if he were ramming his head against the shirt-front. But then we saw blood spurting out. Willy had his mouth wide open. . . .'

*

'No!' Jef Lombard pleaded suddenly. He had got up and was looking at Belloir, dumbfounded.

Van Damme was once more flat up against the wall, his shoulders hunched.

But nothing could have stopped Belloir, not even if he had wanted to himself. It was growing dark. Their faces looked grey.

'Everyone was rushing about,' the voice went on. 'Klein was hunched up, a knife in his hand, and gazing in horror at Willy who was staggering about. These things never happen the way people imagine. I can't explain. . . .

'Mortier didn't fall. Yet the blood was pouring out of the hole in his shirt-front. I'm nearly sure he said:

'"Swine!"

'He just stood there, his legs slightly apart, as if to keep his balance. If it hadn't been for the blood, you'd have said he was the one who was drunk.

'He had big eyes. Just then, they seemed even bigger. He was gripping the button of his dinner-jacket with his left hand. With his right, he was feeling the seat of his trousers.

'Someone yelled in terror. I think it was Jef. We saw Willy's right hand slowly drawing a revolver from his pocket. A small, black, very hard, steel object.

'Klein was rolling on the floor, in the throes of a fit. A bottle fell down and was smashed.

'Willy wouldn't die. He was swaying imperceptibly. He looked at each of us in turn. He couldn't have been seeing straight. He raised his revolver. . . .

'Then someone went forward to grab the gun from him, slipped in the blood and they rolled together on the floor.

'They must have struggled a bit. Because Mortier wouldn't die, do you see? His eyes, those big eyes remained wide open!

'He was still trying to shoot. He kept on saying:

'"Swine!"

'The other fellow must have gripped his throat. In any case, he hadn't much longer to live.

'*I got in an awful mess, as the dinner-jacket lay there on the floor.*'

*

Van Damme and Jef Lombard were now staring in horror at their companion. Belloir continued:

'It was my hand that was round his neck! I was the one who slipped in the pool of blood!'

He was standing in the same place as he was then. But

now he was clean and neat, his shoes spotless and his suit well brushed.

He was wearing a large gold signet ring on his white, well-cared-for right hand, with its manicured nails.

'We stood there as if stunned. We put Klein to bed. He wanted to go and give himself up. No one spoke. I can't explain why. Yet I was perfectly clear in my mind. I can only repeat that people have the wrong ideas about such things. I dragged Van Damme out on to the landing and we whispered together. Klein never stopped struggling and yelling.

'The church-clock struck, but I don't know what time it was, as three of us went down the alleyway, carrying the body. The Meuse was in flood. There were eighteen inches of water on the Quai Sainte-Barbe and the current was very strong. The sluice-gates were open both up- and downstream. In the light of the nearest street-lamp, we could just see the dark lump being swept away by the current.

'My suit was torn and blood-stained. I left it in the studio and Van Damme went and fetched me some clothes. Next day, I spun some yarn to my parents.'

'Did you all meet again?' Maigret inquired slowly.

'No. We left the rue du Pot-au-Noir in confusion. Lecocq d'Arneville stayed with Klein. Since then, we avoided each other, by mutual consent. When we met each other in town, we looked the other way.

'It so happened that Willy's body, thanks to the flood, was not recovered. He had always avoided talking about his connexions with us. He wasn't proud of being a friend of ours. People thought he'd run away. Then the inquiries shifted elsewhere, to low haunts where they thought he might have ended the night.

'I was the first to leave Liège, three weeks later. I broke off my studies abruptly and told my people that I wanted to go on with my career in France. I became a bank clerk in Paris.

'It was through the papers that I learnt that Klein had

hanged himself, the following February, on the door of Saint-Pholien.

'One day, I met Janin in Paris. We didn't mention the incident. But he told me that he, too, had settled in France.'

'I stayed on alone in Liège,' Jef Lombard muttered, looking down.

'You drew hanged men and church steeples,' Maigret retorted. 'Then you drew sketches for the newspapers. Then . . .'

He recalled the house in the rue Hors-Château, the windows with the small greenish panes, the fountain in the courtyard, his young wife's portrait, the photo-engraver's workshop, where posters and pages of newspapers were gradually encroaching on the walls covered with hanged men. . . .

And the kids. The third who had been born the previous day.

Ten years had slipped by, and gradually, everywhere, life had begun to carry on as before, with comparative ease.

Like the two others, Van Damme had wandered about Paris. Chance had taken him to Germany. His parents had left him some money. He had become an important business-man in Bremen.

Maurice Belloir had made a fine marriage. He had reached the top of the ladder.

Vice-chairman of a bank. A fine new house in the rue de Vesle. His boy learning the violin.

In the evenings, he played billiards with well-known figures like himself in the comfortable room in the Café de Paris.

Janin made do with chance female acquaintances, earned his living by making dummies, and, when his day was done, sculpted busts of his mistresses.

Lecocq d'Arneville had got married. Hadn't he a wife and child in the herbalist's in the rue Picpus?

Willy Mortier's father went on buying, cleaning and

selling lorry-loads and wagon-loads of intestines, subsidizing municipal counsellors and feathering his nest.

His daughter had married a cavalry officer and, when the latter did not wish to go into the business, Mortier had refused to hand over the agreed dowry.

The couple lived somewhere in a small garrison town.

CHAPTER II

The Stump of Candle

IT was nearly dark. Their faces stood out against the murky background; their features looked sharper.

As if the semi-darkness had put him on edge, Lombard said nervously:

'Let's have some light!'

There was still a stump of candle in the lamp which had been hanging from the same nail there for years, along with the battered divan, the piece of cretonne, the broken skeleton and the sketches of the girl with the naked breasts, all kept there as security by the owner, who had never been paid.

Maigret lit it and coloured shapes danced on the walls, projected by the red, yellow, and blue glass, like a magic lantern.

'When did Lecocq d'Arneville come and see you for the first time?' the Inspector asked, looking at Maurice Belloir.

'It must have been about three years ago. I wasn't expecting it. The house you saw had just been finished. My boy had barely started to walk.

'I was struck by his resemblance to Klein. Not so much physically as morally. The same consuming fever. The same morbid nervousness.

'He came as an enemy. He was embittered.... Or desperate. I can't find the exact word.

'He sneered, talked sardonically, pretended to admire my house, my position, my life and character. Yet I felt he was ready to burst into tears, like Klein when he was drunk.

'He thought that I had forgotten. He was wrong. I simply wanted to live. Do you understand? That was why I had worked like a slave. Just so as to live.

'He hadn't been able to. It was true that he had lived with

Klein for two months after that Christmas night. We had left. They had stayed on, in this room, in . . .

'I can't explain how I felt about Lecocq d'Arneville. After so many years, I found him just the same as he was before.

'It was as if life had carried on for some and stopped for others.

'He told me he had changed his name, because he didn't want to have anything around that reminded him of the horrible incident. He'd even changed his way of life. He hadn't opened a book since.

'He'd got it into his head to start a new life for himself, as a manual worker.

'I had to read this between the lines, because it was all flung at me with a mass of caustic comments, reproaches, and monstrous accusations.

'He'd failed, he'd made a mess of everything. But part of him was still bound up here.

'It was the same for all of us, I think. But not so intense. Not to that painful, unhealthy degree.

'I think Klein's face haunted him even more than Willy's.

'Married, with a child, he had some bad times. He went on the bottle. He was incapable, not only of being happy, but even of enjoying a moment of peace.

'He told me that he had adored his wife, and that he had left her because, when he was with her, he felt as if he were stealing.

'Stealing happiness. Happiness stolen from Klein. And the other man.

'I've thought about it a lot since, mind you. I think I've understood. We were playing with terrible ideas, with mysticism and morbidity.

'It was only a game. A kid's game. But at least two of us had got caught up in it. The two most fanatical.

'Klein and Lecocq d'Arneville. There'd been talk of killing. Klein wanted to do it. And then he killed himself.

Lecocq, horrified, his nerve gone, dragged this nightmare around with him for the rest of his life.

'The others and myself tried to escape and come to terms with normal life again.

'Lecocq d'Arneville, on the other hand, flung himself body and soul into his remorse, with the fury of despair. He had wrecked his life. He had wrecked his wife's and son's lives.

'Then he turned on us. That was why he came to see me. I didn't understand straight away.

'He looked at *my* house, *my* family, and *my* bank. I saw plainly that he thought it his duty to destroy it all.

'To avenge Klein. To avenge himself. . . .

'He threatened me. He had kept the suit with its stains and tears. It was the only material evidence of what happened that Christmas Eve.

'He asked me for money. A lot! Afterwards, he asked me for more.

'It was our Achilles' heel. All our positions, Van Damme's, Lombard's, mine, even Janin's, depended on money.

'A new nightmare had begun. Lecocq had not miscalculated. He went from one to the other, hawking that sinister suit of clothes round with him. With diabolical accuracy, he worked out just how much to ask for, so as to make things awkward for us.

'You saw my place, Inspector. Well, the house is mortgaged. My wife thinks her dowry is in the bank and untouched. There's not a sou left. And I did other things I shouldn't have.

'He went twice to Bremen to see Van Damme. He came to Liège.

'He was still embittered, still bent on destroying even anything that resembled happiness.

'There had been six of us round Willy's corpse. Klein was dead. Lecocq was living in a constant nightmare. So we all had to be equally miserable. He didn't even spend the money. He lived as poorly as ever, like the time when he used to share a few sous' worth of sausage with Klein. He burnt the notes!

'Yet each of those burnt notes implied fantastic difficulties for us.

'For three years we've been struggling, each in his own town, Van Damme in Bremen, Jef in Liège, Janin in Paris, and myself in Rheims.

'For three years we hardly dared to write to each other, and then Lecocq plunged us back, against our will, into the atmosphere of the *Companions of the Apocalypse*.

'I've a wife. So has Lombard. We have kids. So we try and stick it out for their sake.

'The other day, Van Damme wired to us that Lecocq had killed himself and told us to meet here.

'We were all here. You arrived. After you left, we found out that it was you who had possession of the blood-stained suit, and that you were hot on the scent. . . .'

'Who stole one of my suitcases at the Gare du Nord?' Maigret inquired.

This time Van Damme replied:

'Janin did. I arrived before you. I was hiding there on one of the platforms.'

They all felt equally tired. The stump of candle would perhaps last another ten minutes, no more.

The Inspector moved carelessly and knocked into the skull which fell down and looked as if it were gnawing the floor.

'Who wrote to me at the Hôtel du Chemin de Fer?'

'I did,' Jef replied, without looking up. 'Because of my little girl. The little girl I haven't seen yet. Van Damme guessed. So did Belloir. Both of them were at the Café de la Bourse.'

'And was it you who fired?'

'Yes. I couldn't go on. I wanted to live. Live! With my wife and kids. So I was watching for you outside. I've fifty thousand francs worth of bills at the moment. Fifty thousand francs that Lecocq d'Arneville burnt. But that's nothing. I'll pay them off. I'll do whatever's necessary. But feeling you there behind us. . . .'

Maigret turned to Van Damme.

'And you kept dashing ahead of me, trying to destroy the clues?'

They were silent. The candle flickered. The light filtering through the red glass of the lamp fell only on Jef Lombard.

Then, for the first time, Belloir's voice faltered.

'Ten years ago, immediately after the . . . the thing, I'd have accepted things,' he said. 'I'd bought a revolver, in case they came to arrest me. But ten years of life. Ten years of effort. Of struggle. And other things to consider: a wife, children . . . I think I could have pushed you into the Marne, too. Or fired at you that night outside the Café de la Bourse. . . .

'Because, in a month, less than that, in twenty-four days, the time-limit comes into force. . . .'

Right in the middle of the silence that followed, the candle suddenly gave a last flicker and went out. They were in complete and absolute darkness.

Maigret did not move. He knew that Lombard was standing to his left, Van Damme was leaning against the wall in front of him, and Belloir less than a pace behind him.

He waited, not even bothering to put his hand in his revolver pocket.

He distinctly felt that Belloir was shaking from head to foot, was gasping in fact. He struck a match and said:

'Shall we go?'

In the light of the flame, his eyes seemed even brighter. All four brushed against each other in the doorway, and then on the stairs. Van Damme stumbled because he had forgotten that there was no banister beyond the eighth step.

The carpenter's shop was closed. Through the curtains in a window, they could see an old woman knitting by the light of a small oil lamp.

'Was it along there?' said Maigret, pointing to the unevenly paved street which led to the embankment, a hundred yards off, where there was a gas lamp in a bracket on
the corner of a wall.

'The Meuse came up to the third house,' Belloir replied.
'I had to go into the water up to my knees so as . . . so as to
let him go with the current.'

They retraced their steps and skirted the new church in
the middle of the waste ground which had still not been
properly levelled.

Suddenly, they were in the town, with passers-by, red
and yellow trams, cars and shop-windows.

To reach the town centre, they had to cross the Pont des
Arches; the fast-flowing river was dashing itself noisily
against the piles.

In the rue Hors-Château, they would be waiting for Jef
Lombard: the workmen, downstairs, among the trays of
acid and the plates that the cyclists from the newspapers
would be asking for; the mother upstairs, with the dear old
mother-in-law, and the little girl with her eyes still closed,
lost in the white sheets of the bed. . . .

And the two older ones, who had to stay quiet in the
dining-room decorated with pictures of hanged men.

And another mother, in Rheims, would be giving her son
a violin lesson, while the maid was polishing all the brass
stair-rods and dusting the china vase with the big green
plant.

Work would be coming to an end in Bremen, in the
office-building. The typist and the two clerks would be
leaving the modern office, and as the electricity was switched
off, the enamel letters: *Joseph Van Damme, Export and Import
Agent* would be plunged in darkness.

Perhaps, in one of the brasseries, where they played
Viennese music, some business-man with a shaven head
would be remarking: 'Hullo! That Frenchman's not
here. . . .'

In the rue Picpus, Madame Jeunet would be selling a

tooth-brush, or a couple of ounces of camomile, its pale leaves crackling in the packet.

The small boy would be doing his homework in the back of the shop.

The four men were walking in step. A breeze had sprung up, and it kept the clouds moving, so that from time to time there was bright moonlight.

Had they any idea where they were going?

They passed in front of a lighted café. A drunken man lurched out.

'I'm expected in Paris,' Maigret said, stopping suddenly.

As the three of them looked at him, not knowing whether to feel happy or desperate, and not daring to speak, he stuffed his hands into his pockets.

'There are five kids involved. . . .'

They were not even sure if they had heard him, because the Inspector had muttered the words to himself between his teeth. Now they could see only his broad back and his black overcoat with the velvet collar receding into the distance.

'One in the rue Picpus, three in the rue Hors-Château, one in Rheims. . . .'

*

After leaving the station, he went to the rue Picpus. There the concierge told him:

'It's not worth going up. Monsieur Janin isn't there. They thought it was bronchitis. But it turned out to be pneumonia, so they took him to hospital. . . .'

He then drove to the Quai des Orfèvres. Sergeant Lucas was there, busy telephoning to some bar-owner who had broken the law.

'Did you get my letter, *vieux*?'

'Is it all over? Did you fix things?'

'Did I hell!'

It was one of Maigret's favourite expressions.

'Did they run away? You know, I was darned worried

by that letter. I nearly made a dash to Liège. What were they? Anarchists? Forgers? A gang of international crooks?'

'Kids!' he murmured.

He threw the suitcase, containing what the German expert, in his long and detailed reports, had called *Clothing B*, into a cupboard.

'Come and have a beer, Lucas.'

'You don't seem too cheerful.'

'What ever gave you that idea, *vieux*? There's nothing funnier than life. . . . Are you coming?'

A few moments later, they were pushing the revolving doors of the Brasserie Dauphine.

Lucas had seldom been so worried. Instead of beer, his colleague swallowed down six Pernods, practically one on top of the other. In spite of this, his voice was not very steady, and there was an unusual misty look in his eyes as he said:

'Do you know something, *vieux*? Ten more cases like this and I'll pack it in. Because it would prove that there's a big fellow up there called God who's got it into his head to do our job for us. . . .'

It's true, though, that when he called the waiter, he did add:

'Don't worry. There won't be ten. . . . What's the news back at H.Q.? . . .'

*Some other Penguin crime
books are described on
the following pages*

Murder's Little Sister

PAMELA BRANCH

C1947

'Did she fall or can we claim she was pushed?' That was the question.

Enid Marley shored up *You* magazine with a column for solving readers' problems. Her own were insoluble: her third husband had opted for a concubine and she wanted him back – badly, for appearances' sake. Suicide, she decided, might inject elastic into him – just a little suicide, not too much. But on the day she put her head in the oven, they were having a 'go-slow' at the gas-works.

Foiled in the home, Miss Marley made her big exit through the office window... and bounced on an awning five storeys below. (So foolish you feel, when that happens.) Then it came back to her: someone had gripped her ankle up there. And that's not suicide, readers: that's going along to be murder.

In short, here's another dish of poisoned soufflé from Pamela Branch, as appetizing as *Lion in the Cellar* or *The Wooden Overcoat*.

' Anyone who can fail to laugh out loud here and there is a sad fellow' – *Guardian*

Courtroom U.S.A. 2

RUPERT FURNEAUX

C1979

By the shamelessness and brutality with which they plotted and carried out the murder of a small boy, Leopold and Loeb ushered in the age of juvenile delinquency. As *Courtroom U.S.A. 2* recounts, these two wealthy teenage psychopaths only escaped the chair through the courage and brilliance of their counsel in court. It was a brilliant defence, too, which freed Harry Hoffman, years after he had been imprisoned wrongfully on what seemed to be damning evidence for shooting a woman. At the retrial the prosecution's case fell apart.

Ruth Snyder's name is perhaps more familiar today than the chilling crime which dubbed her 'the bloody blonde'. Rupert Furneaux includes here a full account of her repeated and ruthless – yet somehow naïve – efforts to be rid of an inconvenient husband. And finally he records the fascinating intricacies of the case against Alger Hiss: What exactly had been his relations with the *Time* editor, Whittaker Chambers? Was he just simply a traitor, this former State Department official, or an innocent sacrificed on the altar of McCarthyism?

Also available:

COURTROOM U.S.A. 1 · C1795